I0532958

A Kiss from

Krampus

An Erotic Christmas Tail

Red Hanner

The Island of Misfit Books

A Kiss from Krampus
An Erotic Christmas Tail

ISBN: 978-0692336649

Cover design by Clovia Shaw

Acknowledgements

Extravagant chocolate-coated gratitude to the lovely and talented Clovia Shaw, who encouraged me to keep writing and provided emergency assistance on all fronts.

Thanks also to the Krampus lovers of Purgatory.

Chapter One

Over The River And Through The Woods

I've always hated Christmas. Or loved Christmas, depending on which grandmother I spent it with. Grandma Ellie or Bettina. My parents died in a car wreck when I was four, and after they died, I split my time between my grandmothers, who lived less than ten miles apart and never spoke to each other. Not that I blamed Gram for avoiding Bettina. Anyone who could avoid her did.

Bettina's last husband, who was not my grandfather, always said, "Oh, she's headstrong." I would have used the word *evil*, but that was probably flavored by the number of Christmases and birthdays and every other special occasion that ever mattered to me that she ruined with her temper tantrums. She was like an overgrown toddler. A screamer, a demander, a burner of Christmas trees. Seriously. The Christmas before I turned fourteen, she lit the tree on fire, because she was bored and no one was paying attention to her. As a budding hostile teenager, how was I supposed to compete with that? I should have been rebelling, but I was the one who had to call the fire department.

Being related to her was like working in a nuclear reactor. The best I could hope for was to limit my exposure. I accomplished this by going to college far away from home. I would have gone to the other side of the world, but then I would have missed my other grandmother too much. In the end, it didn't matter how far away I went, because Bettina would have her way.

True to form, she managed to ruin one last Christmas by dying.

She sent a telegram. That's how she lured me back, just four days before Christmas, with a telegram.

Your Grandmother Bettina is dying STOP Her last wish is to see you again STOP

In this day and age, who sends telegrams? People who thrive on drama, that's who. Rich old women who thrill to the prospect of you being accosted in a packed auditorium where you're supposed to be proctoring an exam, only to be presented with an urgent telegram about your grandmother's impending death. Standing there with an audience of two hundred curious freshmen, all I could think was that at least she didn't send a singing telegram.

I wouldn't have gone, except that cutting ties with Bettina had made me a poor grad student. I hadn't been planning to go see Grandma Ellie for Christmas, because I couldn't afford to. Bettina paid for my plane ticket. First class, of course.

Gram picked me up at the airport and dropped me off at Bettina's house. Part of me had wanted to wait, to see if she would die before I had to see her. The other part of me wanted to get it over with. I would see her and then I wouldn't go again. Ever. Telegrams or no. Inheritance or no. Family or no.

"Just like when you were little. I always hated having to drop you off here," Gram said. Probably because I sat there hugging my messenger bag, not wanting to get out of the car.

"Do you think this is a trick?"

"I'm sure it is, but not the kind you mean. From what Father Dalton says, she is dying. All those Sobranies finally caught up with her."

"Father Dalton came to see her?" I said. Bettina was a Catholic only by a serious stretch of the imagination.

"Just to toy with him, that's what I heard. Dangle the possibility of a big tithe and then yank it away."

"And you think that's what kind of trick she's going to play on me?"

"There's a good chance."

I sat there a little longer, then leaned over and hugged Gram before I got out of the car.

"Call me when you're ready to leave," she said.

I nodded and started toward the house. Fat, wet snowflakes pelted me as I ran up the drive and mounted the marble steps. From the outside, the house looked like a cheerful version of the Bates mansion in *Psycho*. On the inside, it was about the same. Everything too opulent and antique, right down to a pair of stuffed pheasants strutting across the parlor mantel. It was immaculately clean, but even an army of maids couldn't get rid of the sour dusty smell of the house.

On the flight, I'd said to myself, "Please let it be quick." Whatever happened, I didn't want it to drag on and on.

3

Surrounded by medical equipment, Bettina looked smaller and older than I remembered. My mother's family had always married young – she was only twenty-two when I was born – but the Holenkranz family was inclined to marry and reproduce late. My father was nearly fifty when he married my mother. *A mismatch made in heaven*, Gram always said. So Gram was only in her sixties, but Bettina was creeping past ninety. Still, she'd never looked old the way she did now. Regardless of how sick she was, her platinum hair was perfectly coifed and she lay back on her throne-like bed, silk brocade covers drawn up over her like armor. Poised for tyranny. When I walked in, her eyes lit up, not so much with pleasure at seeing me, but with desperation.

She really was dying.

"You came," she whispered.

"You asked so I came." I kept my bag on my shoulder and didn't step any further into the room. The last time I let her trick me into hugging her, she told me how unkempt my hair looked and yanked out a handful. It didn't look any better today.

"I asked before and you never came."

"You never sent a telegram before," I said and shrugged.

She laughed, and I had to give her that: she always let me be bad. Maybe that's not a saving grace, but she always laughed when I misbehaved. I was never punished for talking back, and I often got rewarded for being bad at school. If it hadn't been for Gram, I would have grown up as spoiled as Bettina.

"Get out," she snarled at the nurse who had shown me into the room.

When we were alone, Bettina didn't motion me closer. Instead she turned her head on the pillow and nodded toward the wall. "The safe."

I'd never known it was there, hidden behind a painting that she claimed was a genuine Vermeer. A dark panel showing peasants in a field. I touched the edges of the frame uncertainly, found it hinged to the right. Behind it, a safe.

She called out the numbers to me, and I opened the heavy steel door with excitement and fear. Would it be her mother's wedding jewelry? A staggering array of diamonds I had seen on a few special occasions, including photos of my mother at her own wedding. Loaned grudgingly for the day, I imagine. Once, when she caught me looking at that picture, Bettina had muttered, "I suppose once I'm dead, these will be yours."

Or would it be a prank? A taxidermied albino squirrel. She gave me one for my ninth birthday, because I said I wanted a pet. It wore a rhinestone collar with a nametag. Snowy. Her cruel pranks tended toward the elaborate.

The safe was full of leather jewelry cases lined in satin. I recognized the big burgundy box that held her favorite necklace made up of pearls the size of marbles, but that wasn't what she wanted.

"The book, you'll want that," she said. There was a brown leather book no bigger than my hand. I took it out and flipped it open. It was handwritten, spidery penmanship in faded brown ink. Very old. Not English. German. Umlauts and the letter that looks like a capital *B*, but sounds like an *s*.

"Don't snoop. Put that back!" Bettina snapped, when she saw what I was doing.

"I thought you wanted it."

"Not now. Later. First, bring me the little wooden casket."

Since I'd gotten in trouble for looking at the book, I carried the wooden box to her in my open palm. It was about the size of a kitchen match box, and on her command, I opened it. Inside were a pair of silver and gold scissors, and an intricate gold cylinder, capped with a ruby cabochon on one end.

"That," she said. "That is the most valuable thing I own. Now it will be yours."

"Um, what is it?"

"Magic."

I had assumed she still had her faculties, but apparently not.

"Keep that safe and you will be able to do whatever you like," she said. "Anything you like. And there will be no consequences for it. You will never be punished. How did you think I had gone on being as wicked as I am?"

I was tempted to answer, "Money," but I kept my mouth shut.

I turned the cylinder over in my hand, trying to figure out what it was. Real gold, finely engraved, and the ruby was bigger than my thumbnail. But magic? No. I gave the cap an experimental twist and it budged a few millimeters.

"No!" Grandmother Bettina shouted. It startled me so badly I nearly dropped the cylinder. "Never open it. Never! It must remain sealed. Do you understand me?"

"Yes, okay. I won't open it."

She was panting, exhausted. "Good, good."

"Is that all you wanted to see me for?"

Laughter led to coughing and she finally choked out, "Oh, that's what you're worried about, of course. Yes, it's yours. All yours. But the rest of it is a trifle. Nothing. This is the only thing of real value. Without price. Keep it safe. Never let anyone else see it. And keep it locked up."

"What is it really?"

She grinned, drool trickling down her chin.

"When I was a little girl, I was ever so sly. It was all there in my nana's book, once I worked out the secret writing. I'd pulled the thread from the fat man's coat the year before, when my brother was still alive. The fat man would let me kiss and cuddle upon him, but then he would scold me. Nothing for me, but oh such gifts for my little brother. 'An angel,' they all said. All the better to send him back to heaven then. To stop them saying, 'Why can't you be good like Werner?' The next year, when the black one came to whip me, I caught him by his beard. Snip with my silver embroidery scissors. Silver is the only thing that can touch him. Snip and I had his power. I–" Bettina coughed hard for several minutes. Then her eyes opened wide and her mouth went slack. I called for the nurse, but I knew Bettina was already dead.

After the nurse called the county coroner, she stood out on the porch smoking. Ready to leave. I felt like a ghoul, but I stayed in the room and looked through the safe. What I wanted was tucked in the back in a heavy linen envelope: her will. I wanted to know

7

if it was a trick. It wasn't. The will had last been updated when I was seventeen, after her eighth husband died. It left everything to me. The house, her money, her jewelry. Enough to pay off my student loans and then some. I was tempted to call Gram with the good news, but that seemed tacky, so I stayed with Grandmother Bettina.

Her room was more cluttered than I'd ever seen it. It wasn't just that every surface was covered with pill bottles and medical stuff, but that it looked as though she'd spent her last hours sending the nurse to bring her things. A row of porcelain statues she liked. They'd once been scattered around the house, but I guess she'd wanted them all in her room once she was stuck in bed. There was a mountain of papers, too, and some photo albums. With nothing else to do, I picked up the nearest album and opened it. Christmas pictures.

As I turned the pages, I tried to figure out what Christmas it was. I couldn't remember a party this big at Bettina's, and it was big. People in fancy clothes milling around drinking and smiling. She always had elaborate decorations, and in the background of the photos were an enormous tree and crystal ornaments and wreaths. Exactly how the house was decorated now. Even though the house was always dolled up for the holidays, I didn't remember any Christmas parties. Then I turned another page in the album and found myself in the middle of the party.

I was all of four years old, in a white lace dress with my frizzy hair tamed into perfect beribboned curls. Probably the first and the last time my hair had ever looked that neat. Little kid me looked off camera distrustfully. Clearly I was supposed to be posing there with the giant tree and the mound of gifts wrapped in glossy paper and satin bows. Probably I was supposed to look happy or excited, but over the course of half a dozen pictures, the photographer never managed to coax a smile.

It's not like I'm a sourpuss. I can be a happy good-time girl at parties, but at that party, my parents were dead. Rather newly dead, which meant either Bettina was indifferent to my four-year-old feelings, or she was actually trying to cheer me up with a party. If I had to guess, I'd come down on the side of indifferent.

I didn't remember the party or the dress or any of it, but on the next page, it all came back. I remembered Santa Claus, and not fondly. Captive in a twenty-year-old photo, he was a perfectly nice looking Santa. A short, chubby man dressed in a quality costume. Luscious red velvet and real ermine collar and cuffs. Glossy black fireman's boots. The beard and mustache must have been fake, because the man wearing them looked too young. The plump, pink cheeks were all his, though. A nice looking Santa and I was terrified of him.

I looked unhappy sitting on his lap, while he smiled pleasantly, talking to scowling baby Moritza in a friendly way. He held me carefully on his lap. Secure, but without groping me. Nothing inappropriate there, so why did he scare me? Enough that I've been put off Santas my whole life.

On the next page, he posed beside Bettina, who puffed away at her gold cigarette holder. Unlike the photos where he was playing Santa, these were taken up close, head and shoulders

9

only. These pictures explained perfectly why I was afraid of him. His eyes. The irises were washed out blue and the whites tinged yellow. That alone wouldn't have been enough to scare me as a kid. It was that his eyes were dead. He smiled for the camera, but his eyes were flat. Chilling. Count on Bettina to hire a scary Santa.

I snapped the album closed and put it back with the others. Picking up the gold cylinder, I turned it over in my hands.

Magic. Don't open it. Do this. Don't do that. I will have my way! Screw that. She was dead. I was done putting up with her.

I wrapped the ruby cap in the hem of my sweater to get enough traction, and twisted.

It gave with a thin, screeching noise.

A warm, familiar smell wafted out of the gold case: pine, orange, and a hint of cloves. I turned over the cylinder and tamped it against my palm to empty it. I was expecting a scroll scribbled full of hoodoo nonsense. *Magic.*

Out fell a clump of glossy black hair, tied up with a red thread. I shivered, wondering whose hair it was and what it was for. I'd gone that far already, so I picked up the scissors. The openings in the handle were so small, they were obviously meant for a child. My fingertips barely fit in them, but the blades were still sharp and dangerously pointy. When I snipped the red thread, I accidently jabbed myself with the point of one blade. A tiny drop of blood welled up on my finger. I ignored it and tugged on the lattice of red thread. When it unraveled, I teased the bundle of hair open, revealing a braid. A marble-sized ivory bead was strung loosely on the end. That was it. There was nothing else in the tube. Just a swatch of hair, a red thread, and a bead.

In the middle of laughing my head off, I might have shed a tear or two. Not that I would miss Bettina, but that she'd been such an awful person. It was almost sad. Nobody had really loved her and she'd made so many people miserable. Her husbands only married her hoping to outlive her and inherit her money.

I was still laugh-crying when I heard the coroner come in the side door. I hurriedly stuffed the wad of hair back in the gold tube and tried to twist the cap back on. It was too tight and I was out of time, so I tossed it on the night table alongside all the pill bottles.

At the doorway to Bettina's room, Digger gave me a hard, back thumping hug. I wasn't put off getting a hug from the county coroner, because he was an old friend of Gram's. I was put off by the sight of his assistant, a kid I went to school with. Danny Diekater, a.k.a. Danny the Dickhead. While I hugged Digger, Danny grinned at me.

"I wasn't expecting to see you, Moritza," Digger said. "Normally, this is the point where I would offer my condolences to the family, but …"

"I know. How are you doing?"

"Oh, my back hasn't given out yet." That was what he always said. I guess it was some kind of gravedigger joke. "If you want to wait outside, we'll get her on her way."

I went into the parlor and sat on the sofa, looking at the stuffed pheasants strutting on the mantel. Whatever else

11

happened, I swore, I was never going to be the kind of rich person who decorated with dead birds. Snowy the Squirrel could be grandfathered in, but that was it. No more dead, stuffed things. Unless I could find somebody to stuff Bettina in the attack pose.

Half an hour later, Danny rolled out the gurney, covered with a white sheet. Digger came after him, patting his coat pockets like he had forgotten something. He stopped in front of me, frowning, and then smiled and squeezed my arm.

"I suppose you'll want me to call Grayson's Funeral Parlor to come pick her up when we've cleared her?"

I hadn't even thought of it, so I nodded.

After Digger and Danny were gone, the nurse left, too, leaving me alone in the house. I went back into the bedroom to sit down and call Gram.

"Is everything okay? Are you …" Her voice faltered.

"I'm okay. The Bettina Noir is – she died." That was our nickname for her. Our own personal *bête noir*.

"Did you see her before?"

"Yes. It wasn't a trick."

Gram sighed heavily. "Oh good. For once she did the right thing. I'm so happy for you, sweetheart."

"Can you come get me, Gram?"

"I'll be there in a jiffy."

After I disconnected, I stood up, intending to go wait in the parlor. The ruby cap winked up at me from the rug. The cylinder lay a few inches away, next to a pill bottle. I'd forgotten all about it, and Digger had probably knocked it off the night table when they were moving the body. I scooped up the cap and the cylinder, and stuffed them in my pocket.

It was after eight already, dark and snowy outside, so I waited inside the front door, looking for the headlights of Gram's car. About when I started to expect her, my phone rang.

"The goddamn car won't start," Gram said. "Your cousin Elliot gets off work at midnight. He says he can come pick you up then. I'm so sorry, sweetie."

"It's okay. It's not a problem."

It wasn't okay. I didn't want to be in that big old house alone. I wanted a drink. A lot of drinks. And a hug. And a long sleep. I could have walked the nine miles. I had before, when I needed to escape from Bettina, but I dreaded going out in the miserable cold and darkness. I felt silly tip-toeing around the house, acting like a stranger when I had slept there half my childhood. Even sillier, I had a safe full of jewelry and not even enough cash to call for a cab. I'd landed at the airport with a whopping six dollars in my purse.

Luckily, in addition to a safe full of jewels, I had a liquor cabinet and a wine cellar that were equally full. So I drank. And drank. An entire a bottle of Chateau Margot, my grandmother's favorite. Then I trudged upstairs to my frilly pink princess room. Bettina picked all the décor, and it looked like a godforsaken cross between Versailles, My Little Pony, and *Flowers in the Attic*. Luckily, some of the clothes I'd abandoned when I left for college were still there, including a soft old cotton t-shirt nightgown. It smelled stale from its years in the drawer, but it was familiar.

Drunk in my childhood bed, I was sound asleep in minutes.

Chapter Two

It Came Upon A Midnight Clear

I woke to a rough hand over my mouth and the smell of pine and oranges and cloves in my nose. Someone was holding me down and trying to turn me over on my stomach. My luck to be there alone on the night somebody decided to break in. I tried to stay calm, to think of what to do.

A hot voice in my ear said, "Now you'll have what you deserve, you little bitch."

He had an accent. German maybe. I bucked hard and tried to force his hand away. His arm was hairy. Every movement he made produced a chinking metal sound. Like chains. Did he plan to chain me up?

"You are not so little now. Not at all," he muttered.

Then I lost the fight for traction and he flipped me onto my stomach. I went with it, used the momentum to haul myself toward the nightstand. I reached for the lamp, planning to clobber him, but he jerked me back before I could reach it.

We wrestled I don't know how long, but I was getting tired and he wasn't. He'd worked my nightgown nearly up to my waist and every time I tried to reach back to hit him or claw him, I snagged myself on something rough and sharp, like thorns. Finally he took his hand off my mouth so that he could hold onto me better, and that stray hand grabbed my breast. At the same moment I screamed, an almost electrical shock jumped between his hand and my chest, like the static from wearing wool socks on a wool rug in the winter.

He grunted and loosened his grip on me. I lunged toward the nightstand, but before I could grab the lamp he closed his hand around my wrist. Still I managed to slam my hand down on the base. The light clicked on and I twisted my head, wanting to at least get a look at him. I wanted to be able to identify him to the police.

That's what I intended, but I'm pretty sure the police would have laughed me right out of the station if I'd given them his description. He wasn't just hairy. He was furry. Black fur covered every part of him. His head, his face, his arms, his chest, even his legs. And he had horns. Curved black corkscrews a good four inches long. He was like a B-movie science experiment. Half man, half goat. It had to be a dream. I'd drunk too much and was having a crazy, very realistic dream. The smell of oranges was intoxicating.

"You're not a little girl!" He stared at me like I was the one with horns. He reached out like he was going to touch my hair, but I jerked my head to keep away from him.

"No, I'm not a little girl!" I yelled over my shoulder at him.

He was still straddling me, his hairy thighs clamped on either side of my waist, but he didn't seem to know what to do. I twisted under him, wanting to have my hands between us to fight him off. Only he wasn't attacking me anymore and he didn't try to stop me from rolling onto my back.

"What are you?" he said.

"What am I? What the hell are you?"

He was staring at my chest and I knew without looking that my nightgown had gotten stretched out of shape and he was staring at my breasts. He brought his hand toward them and I realized the electrical shock had come from him. His surprise. He stopped short of touching me, his hand hovering over my skin. I felt the charge there, making the fine hairs around my nipple stand up. Then to my squirming horror, my nipple went hard.

His eyes, which had been glittering black and angry, softened. He drew his hand back.

"Child's hair, but not a child. You should be a child," he said.

"I'm not a child, so let me go, you fucking pedophile."

He frowned. "What is a fucking pedophile?"

"A sick creep who wants to have sex with a child."

"With a child? Who would do such a thing with those nasty, snot-faced little monsters? They're worse than elves."

He looked so disgusted that I almost laughed. He'd broken into my house, planning to do God knows what to me, but even he had his standards.

"What are you? And how did you get into my house?" I said.

"I am Krampus. And it is my right to come here. And it is not your house. This is the problem. You are not her. I am searching for that evil little girl, Bettina von Holenkranz, the one who

17

clipped my beard. Her ward charm has been broken and now she shall have her punishment."

Definitely a dream. That's what happens when you have a long, stressful day and go to bed on an empty stomach after drinking a whole bottle of Bordeaux.

"Bettina was my grandmother and she's dead. She died today."

"Dead? Dead?" With a disappointed sigh he sank back on his haunches, settling his weight across my hips. All he wore was that pelt of black fur. It was thick and shaggy enough to cover him, but I was sure I felt some unmentionable part of him resting against my belly.

"You are sure she is dead?"

"Yes, she's dead."

"And I was going to give her such a whipping," he hissed. "Such a whipping she would never forget it."

"Somebody should have given her a whipping."

"Yes, precisely. A terrible whipping with a good bundle of birches."

It had fallen to the side, the bundle of twigs that had scratched me, but he picked it up and brandished it with a malevolent and very white smile. He was almost a handsome figment of my imagination from that angle. If you went in for devilish eyebrows and sharp aquiline noses. And lots of black fur. And horns.

"And so the whipping must come due to you!"

He leapt up, his feet planted on either side of my hips, and flipped me on to my belly again. When the bundle of twigs hit

18

my ass, my nightgown wasn't enough to protect me. I would have tried to escape, except as I went to get on my hands and knees to get away, I saw he didn't have feet at all. He had hooves. Neat little black goat hooves. That stopped me in my tracks.

Swoosh! SMACK! The birches hit me again with burning accuracy. I yelped and lunged off the bed. He jumped after me, his hooves clicking on the wood floor. He grabbed a handful of my nightgown, so I turned and slammed my head into his belly. It filled my nose with the smell of Christmas again.

"Ooof," he said, falling back on the bed, dragging me with him, my nightgown pulled up over my head.

"What do you want?"

"I want my beard, which she stole from me!"

"Fine! Take it! It's right here!"

He let go of me long enough for me to wrench my nightgown back into place. I reached for the cylinder on the nightstand, but in the fighting it had rolled off onto the floor, so I got down on my knees to look for it.

"It was right here. Bettina gave it to me."

"So *you* unraveled the thread from the old elf's coat?"

"She told me not to open it, but I did."

"Why?" he wondered from above me. I had my head under the bed, looking for the cylinder and so it seemed safe to answer honestly.

"Because anything she thought was important, I didn't want. She was – she made me so unhappy. She said not to open the case, so I did. To not be like her."

19

"Ah," he said. "She was a very wicked girl. You perhaps are not."

"I'm not."

I slithered out from under the bed, with the capless cylinder in one hand.

Krampus was sitting on the edge of the bed, with a small leather book in his hand, peering at it. For a second I thought it was Bettina's book, but it was much thicker.

"Moritza Holenkranz, yes? Born on February 29, 1988?" he said.

"How did you–" Stupid. He'd probably looked in my purse while I was passed out.

"1988? This is true? That is the year of your birth?"

"Yes, it's true."

"So many years lost." He put a hand to his head like it hurt. For a few moments, he stayed like that, not saying anything. Then he looked at his book again. "Mostly good. A few infractions, but nothing to bring you to my attention, but then not so good as to bring you to Herr Klaus's attention, either." He shot me a wicked smile and added a wink. "Not so good as that."

"Herr Klaus?" I wasn't sure I wanted to know.

"Herr Klaus. The old fat elf. Kris Kringle. St. Nick."

"Who brings toys to all the good girls and boys?"

He laughed. Hairy devil goat-man threw back his head and laughed. The sound was strangely goat-like but too heavy on the bass. Still laughing, he tucked the leather book into his satchel.

20

Before he closed the flap, I saw a length of heavy chain coiled inside and what looked like an orange.

"Not all. Only to the very best boys and girls. The very special ones. Just as I come to punish only the very worst. Not the naughty ones. The evil ones."

"Here's your beard," I said.

I felt a little headachy. Drunk and hungover at the same time. Whatever he was – hallucination or devil – I wanted him to go. If only I could keep that delicious Christmas smell.

Without even a thank you, he snatched the cylinder out of my hand and emptied it into his palm. For an instant, he wore a ridiculously happy, goatish smile, and then he scowled.

"*Nein*!"

"That's the only beard Grandmother Bettina gave me, so if it's not yours–"

"*Wo ist mein Schmuckstück?*" he roared.

"Your what?"

"My trinket!"

Between his delicate hooves and his impish smile, I'd started to think of him as mostly harmless. But he stood up and I realized he was a head taller than me and broad in the shoulders. A big man, strong enough to throw me down on the bed. I was mostly scared by the thought, but there was a small, sneaking sliver of me that was excited by the prospect. I've always been a big girl. Tall and muscular, cursed by short skinny boyfriends. I could do a fireman's carry on my last boyfriend, Greg. He couldn't pick me up at all.

"Where is my trinket?" Krampus said.

"The bead?"

"Yes, carved of reindeer horn."

Of course. Naturally, it was carved out of reindeer horn.

"It was in there," I said, but I could see it wasn't in his hand. With all the wrestling it must have come loose when the cylinder fell off the night table. "It must be under the bed somewhere."

I started to get down and look for it but he was already crawling under the bed. I got another jolt to see that he had a long, swishing black tail. Mesmerized by the sight of it whipping back and forth in agitation, I sat down and waited for him to find the bead. Waited for him to go back to the North Pole or wherever.

"So you live at the North Pole?" I said.

"No, not with those filthy elves."

"Are elves really that filthy? They look so cute in the movies."

"Nasty creatures. Almost as bad as children."

His tail flicked against my bare ankle, jolting me to attention. As alert as I would be if a lion walked into my room and brushed its tail against my leg. I needed to be that alert, because he still counted as a dangerous, wild animal in my book. A very eloquent wild animal. The tail returned, almost curiously, and stroked against my ankle. I moved my leg out of his reach.

"Don't you ever wear clothes?" I said.

"Why would I need clothes?"

"Isn't it cold at the North Pole?"

"Did I not say that I do not live there? You are not a child, yet you ask questions like a child."

"Sorry."

He went on searching under the bed, muttering and saying things in German. It sounded like cursing.

"Where is it?" he shouted and wriggled out from under the bed. He knelt there beside me, his head on the edge of the bed, breathing hard. His eyes were dark and liquid, like he was about to cry.

"Is it that important?"

"Yes. For as long as she had bound my beard I was not free to do my work. The charm is unraveled, but without my trinket, I am almost powerless. I must have it back."

"I'm sorry. I know it has to be here. It was when I went to sleep. We'll find it."

I've always had a soft spot for strays. Just like that I went from potential rape victim to Good Samaritan. He seemed so forlorn I wasn't even scared of him. I reached out and tentatively patted the spot between his horns. He sighed and scooted his head closer, so I petted him some more.

After a few minutes, he nestled his head up on my leg, the way a dog will, his horns coming dangerously close to my belly. Still, I went on petting him. I'd expected his fur to be coarse, but it was silky fine and whispered through my fingers so pleasantly that I ran my hand over his head and down to the back of his neck. The fur there was so inviting that I gave him a *scritch-scritch*. Like I thought I was at a petting zoo.

23

"Such kindness. You are certainly not a child," he whispered. When he nuzzled against my leg, I thought he wanted me to pet him some more.

Abruptly, where I had my hand on his neck, the hair stood up, and a shudder ran down his spine.

"What is that smell?" he said.

"I thought that was you. That orangey, Christmas tree smell?"

"No. That is me. This smell is you."

He shifted his head under my hand and pressed his whole face between my legs, so that I had to lean back on the bed to avoid getting jabbed by his horns. When he exhaled it was like a furnace on my crotch, heating my chilled thighs. Heating more than just my thighs.

"Yes, that is you. And such a smell it is, too."

"Jeez, I've been traveling since five this morning and I haven't had a shower since then. So I'm a little ripe. Back off."

I pushed at him, but he didn't go. I tried to scoot back on the bed, but he grabbed me behind the knees and pulled me closer. The movement rucked my night gown up to my thighs and with a quick push, he shoved it the rest of the way up. Then his face was pressed right into my crotch, breathing onto my landing strip of pubic hair.

"So this is what human women smell like. I always wondered," he mumbled against me.

"Why? What do your women smell like?"

"I have no women. And elven women smell like damp straw and gingerbread."

24

"No women?" That seemed sadder to me than him losing his beard trinket. "How were you born then?"

"That was so long ago. I do not remember."

He rubbed his palms against my thighs and closed his eyes, as he nuzzled closer to me. I pushed against his horns, but not hard enough to budge him. I couldn't figure out how to get him off me without being unkind. I couldn't bring myself to yell at him. Or kick him. Or any of the things that would probably stop him.

Except that it felt so nice I didn't really want it to stop. I wanted it to feel nicer. Wondering what he would do, I opened my knees a little wider. He wiggled his face, chin first and slipped further between my thighs, his beard and sideburns rubbing against my legs. When I opened them more, he growled and tightened his hands on my thighs, sharp black claws at the tips of his fingers digging into my plumpness. The sensation was scary and exciting at the same time. Like I couldn't make up my mind, I pushed against his horns, but when he pushed back I let my legs open wider. Half an inch more and he was nose to nose with my clit.

I wasn't sure if he would know what to do. And if he didn't, whether I would be brave enough to suggest it. Without me even saying a word, though, he opened his mouth and unfurled the most amazing tongue I'd ever seen. A thing to put Gene Simmons to shame: long, brilliant red, with a clever, curling tip. Possibly prehensile.

Like it was an experiment, he made a tentative slurp and rolled his tongue in his mouth, like he was tasting wine.

25

"Hmmmmmmmm." He breathed out against me, and then his tongue returned for further investigation. At first I lay back with my eyes closed tight. Strictly childhood delusion. If I couldn't see him, he couldn't see me. And if I didn't look at him, I wouldn't have to think about what he was. Not human.

Then he started working that wicked red tongue against me. It ran long laps up my labia before he thrust it into me, where it seemed to get thicker and then thinner, almost pulsing. He withdrew and made his tongue slither in tight corkscrews around and around my clit. When I moaned, he made a pleased little grunt of discovery. After that I didn't care whether Krampus looked at me. I opened my legs wide and, half-crazy with pleasure, grabbed onto his horns to steer him back to my clit. He laughed at that, deep in his throat, and held tight to my thighs. Drawing my clit into his mouth, he sucked on it at the same time he danced his tongue over it.

I've never been completely comfortable with cunnilingus, especially with anybody new. I make a mess. It's never a simple orgasm. If it's any good, it's gushing wet, and that always makes me hold back. By the time I got there with him, I didn't care. I arched my back, held him tight to me, and let myself explode into his mouth. He didn't even stop licking me. In fact, he licked me harder with stinging darts of his tongue, and all that slippery wet adding to the pleasure of it. The second orgasm came so hot on the heels of the first, I almost didn't understand what it was. That had never happened. But with his tongue curling up into my pussy, pressing hard around the curve that hid my g-spot, I moaned and thrashed, my hands going limp and my legs quivery from the aftershocks.

Gasping, I lay still for a moment thinking, *What have I done?* Let some strange goat-man eat my pussy. Was I supposed to return the favor? Shouldn't I? Wasn't that the polite thing to do?

I scooted backwards on the bed, not sure what would happen, and he followed on his knees. He knelt over me, staring at me, with all the fur on his face wet and rumpled. He looked as surprised as I felt. His gaze drifted from mine, down to himself.

I finally got up my nerve to look and saw that he could have used some pants right about then. Out of all that thick fur had emerged his cock. It was thick and red, damp looking. Obscene. As obscene as his tongue and just as impressive. I wasn't an expert on penises, but his was bigger than Greg's or Scott's, my boyfriend before Greg. Those were really the only two I knew anything about.

My first thought was to have it in me. Considering what he was, I could roll over onto all fours and present myself to him rump first. Let him mount me like an animal.

I was shocked at myself. Not just for thinking of it that way, but for thinking of it at all. That would be crazy. The last person I had sex with was Greg, and that was so long ago, I wasn't on the Pill anymore, and I wasn't about to get knocked up with a goat baby. It would have to be tit for tat. I'd have to suck him off. I was trying to decide how to approach it when I heard a car honk outside. Krampus' eyes darted toward the window, and I may have thought I was dreaming, but he looked like he'd just woken up.

"*Verfluchen mich für einen Esel*," he said.

His cock didn't so much wilt as it retreated into his fur.

When my phone rang, I scrabbled for it and answered.

"Hey, cuz! It's Elliot. Get on out here and I'll take you up to Gram's."

I'd intended to call her and tell her I could spend the night at Bettina's, but with the wine I'd forgotten. After I told Elliot I was coming down, I looked around for my clothes.

Krampus stood next to the bed, watching me. I looked up at him. I was a flat six feet tall, so he had to be at least 6'6". In hooves.

"I have to go. My cousin's here to pick me up."

"My trinket." He frowned and I remembered that moment between his anger and my pleasure, when he'd been so sad and anxious. Whatever he was, Bettina had caused him a lot of problems.

"I can look for it tomorrow. It's got to be here. It must have just rolled away somewhere. A crack in a floorboard or something. I'll find it for you. I can leave it for you. On the mantel downstairs, there's a–"

"I will come back. When you find it, I will come back to get it."

He shouldered his satchel and picked up his bundle of twigs. Striding toward the bedroom door, like he was going to walk out, he vanished.

Feeling out of my body, I pulled my clothes on, and hurried downstairs to get in Elliot's truck. We hugged each other over the armrest, and as he drove, I stared out the windshield into the snow.

"–Santa Claus on Saturday," Elliot said.

I jumped in my seat and blurted out, "What about Santa Claus?"

"Are you listening to anything I've said?"

"I'm just a little distracted. That's all. With Bettina."

"Yeah, but it's good you're finally shut of her. So she just wanted to see you before she died, huh?"

"So what about Santa Claus?" I said.

"Oh, I took the girls to see the mall Santa on Saturday. Tiffany had a list about as long as my arm and Kimmi cried like he was going to eat her."

The phrase "eat her" caught me up, and I was glad it was dark, so Elliot couldn't see I was blushing. As much as I wanted to believe it had all been some crazy drunk dream, I was wet between the legs the way I only got when I came. Whatever it – he was, he had completely pushed my buttons.

"So are you?" Elliot said.

"What? I'm sorry."

"Are you staying for the Christmas party?"

"Yeah. There's the funeral. I have to figure that out. And I might as well stay, since I'm already here."

"Cool. It'll be fun, like old times."

29

I wasn't sure if I wanted it to be like old times. When I was in high school, Elliot had often invited me and my friends to his house to party. He'd been so exciting back then. My older cousin with his fast car and his own place and he always treated us. Paid for the booze, paid for dinner. Once or twice, I think we almost did something. A wrestling match on his king size water bed that went a little too far. A slow dance in his kitchen after everyone else had passed out. Both of us drunk, so that the next morning I could act like nothing had come close to happening. I'm too practical, I guess. It wasn't like you could really have a relationship with your cousin, so better not to get anything started. Plus, I was an only child. I'd wanted a brother more than I wanted a cousin with benefits.

"–still dating him?"

"What?"

"Jeez, Moritza!"

"I'm sorry. I'm really tired."

"It's okay. We're almost there. I bet Gram's got your bed made up for you."

She did. While I was at Bettina's, Gram had unpacked my suitcase and laid out a nightgown for me. After I changed and brushed my teeth, she even tucked me in, petting my hair over my pillow. I always loved that, having her touch my hair, but that night all I could hear was the sharp German sounds of a goat-man saying, "Child's hair, but not a child." My hair had always been baby fine.

Chapter Three

Twas The Night Before Christmas

It started out as a perfect Christmas Eve. I woke up to the smell of Gram baking in the kitchen, getting ready for the party. She made pancakes and hot chocolate for me. Still in my pajamas, I ate in her too small kitchen with the sun streaming in through the frosted windows. Just like when I was a little kid, she had homemade paper chains and snowflakes hanging from the ceilings.

It would have been a perfect Christmas Eve, except for Bettina being such a bitch she had to die before Christmas. Instead of spending the day with Gram, I was going to spend it making the arrangements for Bettina's funeral. I had to meet with her lawyer, and then with the funeral director, and then I needed to go back to her house to pick out clothes.

Don't forget to look for the goat-man's beard trinket, a voice said in my head. Right. I decided I'd better plan on it not being a hallucination. If he came back looking for that bead, I wanted to be sure I had it.

"Gram, have you heard of Krampus?" I said.

She was bent over, checking on cookies in the oven. Her voice echoed back toward me menacingly: "Krrrrrampusss." She said it the same way he had, with the thick *r* and the soft *a*. "St. Nick's helper. He supposedly punishes bad kids. Oh and puts the orange in the toe of your Christmas stocking."

"Really? Really?"

Gram stood up, laughing. "Yes, really. Why?"

"I just never heard of him before."

"Well, he's not popular anymore, the way Santa is. But you know your great-grandparents were Old Country. Very Austrian. My mother always threatened that Krampus was going to come whip us if we didn't behave." Gram put on a stern frown and intoned in her mother's voice: "If you don't do as Mama says, Krampus vill come und gif you zuch a vhipping."

My nape hair prickled uneasily. Surely, Gram had told me that before. That had to be why it was so familiar.

Gram bent over me to give me a hug, and I gave it back to her gratefully. As she stood up, she said, "Is that some new lotion? I love the orange, but the pine is awfully masculine."

"I'm going to take my shower and go up to Bettina's. The sooner I get it all taken care of, the better."

"Good girl. Everyone's coming at six and we'll eat at seven."

I scrubbed myself down with plenty of hot water and Gram's rose petal soap, and headed to the lawyer's office to go over paperwork. That took until noon and then I went to the funeral parlor. I basically said, "She loved red. Red everything." The lawyer said all the expenses would be covered, so there was no mention of cost. Whatever casket the funeral director suggested, I said, "Yes. Perfect." The lining packages. The this, that, and the other packages. Flowers, yes. Red roses.

After all, I wasn't sure anyone but me would be at the service, so perhaps no one else would send flowers. Even with me saying yes to everything – concrete vault, something something sealant – it took hours. There was so much fuss and formality, and I still had to go and pick out clothes. And provide a recent photograph for hair and makeup styling. I got the deluxe package on that.

Back at the house, I started with the clothes, digging through the racks in Bettina's dressing room. I picked out a sumptuous silk charmeuse evening gown in blood red. To counterpoint, I added a black mink bolero jacket. Like she was going to the opera instead of the grave. Then I stepped into her bedroom to look through the jewelry in the safe. I had the oddest tingle when I did. The painting was closed over the safe, but not latched, and when I reached for the safe handle, it was locked. Had I done that?

As stupid as it was, I was pretty sure that although I'd latched the painting securely, I'd left the safe door closed but unlocked. I'd been afraid I wouldn't remember the combination. I'd pushed the door shut and closed the painting. Who had been in the house besides me? Surely Digger wouldn't – no. The nurse? No, she hadn't been in the room alone. After trying a couple of variations on Bettina's birthday, I hit on the combination. I'd remembered the numbers, but not the order. Everything in the safe was jumbled. When I'd taken out the will, the box of pearls had been on top. Now it was shuffled down near the bottom. Crap.

I stood there trying to decide what to do. Should I call the police? Would there be a point? What was I going to say? *Um, I don't know if anything's missing, but stuff has been moved around.* I pulled out a handful of things and found the amazing diamonds and the giant pearls. All the things I knew of that were valuable. All accounted for.

I opened a few more boxes until I found the earrings and choker that were made of stripes of onyx and ruby. I'd always thought it was hideous, so why not bury it with her? After all I was sending her off wearing several thousand dollars' worth of fur. Bonus: maybe PETA would show up to protest her funeral and I wouldn't be there alone.

Then I remembered the little book. The one she'd gotten so snippy about. It was gone.

I stepped back from the safe and looked around the room, like I was suddenly going to see a clue, an answer to the mystery. All I saw was that it was neater than it had been the night before.

So someone had broken in, left maybe a million dollars in diamonds in an open safe, then straightened up before they walked out with an old diary written in German. That didn't make any sense.

After standing there for another ten minutes, taking out my cell phone, thinking about calling the police, and then putting it away, I decided I didn't care. I locked the safe, gathered up the clothes I'd picked and carried them out to Gram's Dodge which I hoped, with the new battery Elliot had put in it, wouldn't strand me. With my worldly obligations taken care of, I went back into the house to see about my otherworldly obligations.

In case I had any doubts about what had happened last night, my bedroom smelled like a bordello on Christmas. Sex and pine boughs. I crawled over every square inch of the floor and found nothing. The bead wasn't there. From a shelf in the corner, Snowy the Squirrel watched the proceedings with his pink glass eyes.

Then I remembered what I'd been too drunk to remember last night. The cap to the cylinder had been off in Bettina's room. The bead must have fallen out there. I hurried back to her room and started searching the floor in there. I shifted the night table, then slithered under the bed. As I was crawling around, I looked back the way I had come and realized that each of my footprints was clearly defined in the rug's pile. There were regular stripes running across it. So the thief had also vacuumed, or the housekeeper stole the book, or the two things were totally unrelated.

"Crap," I said. "Crap crap crappity crap."

Did I even know where the vacuum was kept? No. I'd never been made to lift a finger at Bettina's house. I didn't even know what drawer the spoons were kept in. I'd always had my Count Chocula brought to me on a tray. With a flower in a vase.

I stormed through the house, yanking open doors until I found the maid's closets. Each one was identical, neatly stocked with various cleaners. On the floor stood a mop bucket, a mop, a broom, and a vacuum. Anyway, on the third floor and the ground floor there was a vacuum. On the second floor, where Bettina's room was, the mop bucket had been scooted to the center, taking up part of the footprint of what should have been a vacuum.

I dragged both vacuums to the scullery to empty the bags, but the bead wasn't in either of them. It was almost dinner time. I was hungry and tired and dusty, and I still needed to get the clothes to the funeral parlor. That space in the second floor closet where a vacuum should have been nagged at me. Vandy Harris had been cleaning Bettina's house almost my entire life. I couldn't imagine she was dragging one of the other vacuums up and down the stairs every day. So where was the vacuum from the second floor?

As I was bent over, putting the empty bags back in the vacuums, I heard a *click-click-click* that was so distinctive I didn't even have to turn around to see who it was. His hooves, clattering on the tile floor.

"You have not found it."

"No. I checked everywhere I might have dropped it. I checked the fucking vacuums to see if it got sucked up. I–"

SMACK! The birch bundle stung even through the seat of my jeans. I jumped up, one hand to my stinging ass, the other in a fist, ready to fight back.

He stood behind me, all black and enigmatic, the birches in his hand.

"You bastard, I'm trying to find your goddamn bead! Why would you do that?"

"Good little girls don't swear."

"I'm not a little girl."

"No, you are not," he said, and the way it sounded, he thought it was a good thing. "But you're small enough to put on my knee."

"Oh my god, you perv. What do you want? Do you want your bead or do you want to fuck me?"

"Both."

"Well, I don't have the bead, and I have a Christmas party to go to, so you're out of luck on both counts. Why don't you go get some elf action?"

"I'd sooner" — he made a rude gesture — "a reindeer."

"Nice."

He made a grumbling, growling sound and smacked the edge of the counter with his birches. *

"Moritza Holenkranz, I need my trinket."

"I got that, okay? I just have other stuff going on. I–"

"I need also … other things." He leaned down when he said it, until his cheek brushed against mine and his breath was hot in my ear. "You smell different. Not as good."

37

"I took a shower."

"Too many flowers, not enough you."

"Well, you smell like Pine-Sol." It wasn't true. God, he smelled like Christmas. Like happy, good Christmas. Confusing as hell.

He brought the tip of his forefinger to my throat. The claw there was sharp, but he only trailed it down my sternum into the front of my shirt. Then the finger started sneaking into the edge of my bra, while his thumb ran across the front of my shirt, searching for my nipple, which shamelessly poked up. He grasped it and gave it a little twist. Not enough to hurt, just enough to send a rush of heat between my legs.

"You must show these to me," he said.

"Show you what?"

"These parts of you that are part of your being a woman."

"I have to go. I'm having dinner with my family."

"Then you will return tomorrow to find my trinket?"

"Tomorrow is Christmas."

"Yes, I know what tomorrow is," he said.

I turned to the side, catching him in the chest with my shoulder, and he stepped back. Although I expected him to try to stop me, I kept walking. Out of the kitchen, out the back door, to where the Dodge was parked in the drive. It started on the first try, and it was just after seven when I pulled up to Gram's house. Most everyone was already there, it looked like. I sat in the dark car for a few minutes to pull myself together.

When I thought I was calmed down, I got out of the car and started up the back walk. About halfway there, I ran smack into what felt like a wall. A wall of fur. Of course, he was nearly invisible in the dark. He caught me before I could fall, but I came up swinging. It was useless, though. I couldn't see him well enough to hit him, and he was laughing at me. That laugh that was almost like a goat bleating, but deep in his throat.

"Did you follow me?" I snapped.

"I have no need to follow you. I knew where you were ."

"Well, you can't come in. My whole family's here."

"You have not said that you will come to find my trinket tomorrow." He was thinking about other things, though, because in the dark, he slipped his arm around my waist and bent his head to sniff my hair.

"Fine. I'll help you find your stupid reindeer bead. Okay?"

The back door swung open and Gram called, "Is that you, Moritza?"

"I'm coming."

The porch light flooded the backyard, spotlighting me and Krampus next to me, satchel swung jauntily over his shoulder, birch whip dangling down.

"Sweet cartwheeling Jesus!" Gram said.

"Shit!" I said. If he gave my grandma a heart attack, I was going to cut off a whole lot more than his beard.

Gram burst out laughing and clapped her hands. "That's why you asked about Krampus! Come inside so I can get a better look. That is the most amazing Krampus costume I've ever seen."

Krampus stepped around me, mincing down the walkway on his hooves. He *clip-clopped* across the porch, right into the kitchen.

"You find me very like him, *mein Frau*?"

"*Ja wohl. Wilkommen, Herr Krampus*."

"*Danke schön*." He bowed to her like an old fashioned dancer. I stepped up behind him, grabbed a handful of the fur on his back and yanked. He didn't make a sound, but he gave me an evil look out of the corner of his eye. A warning look. *Don't cross the man with the birch whip*.

"Your German's not half bad," Gram said.

"I should think not. My English, too, also *sehr gut*, no?"

"Oh!" Gram said. "Are you really German? Where are you from?"

"Bayern."

Gram squealed with excitement. When she reached for his hand, he let her take it. Before I could stop them, she pulled him after her, leading him toward the crowded front room, where she presented him: "Look! A real Bavarian Krampus!"

Everyone marveled and gasped and went on and on about his amazing costume. Oh sure, with the wonders of modern monster make-up, the horns, the furry body suit, maybe even the tail, weighted to make it swish convincingly. No one seemed to notice the sheer impossibility of a man his size balanced on those tiny hooves.

Then my Uncle Dean came out of the back bedroom in his Santa Claus suit. It was adequate at best: red velour trimmed in once-white fake fur, with a glaringly fake beard. Nothing like Bettina's Santa.

Krampus made a big deal out of the introduction.

"Ah, old St. Nick. We have a night of work ahead of us, don't we?" he said.

"Ho ho ho. Yes, we do." Uncle Dean was putting on a show for the little cousins. Krampus was putting on a show for me.

"You old elf, you have lost some weight at last, I see."

"Ahahaha. I've been, uh, trying to cut back on the cookies."

"I think it was laziness and not sweets which puffed you up," Krampus said.

"Come on, come on," Aunt Sheila said. "Let's get pictures with the kids."

So we did. All the kids filed through to sit on Santa's lap, while Krampus menaced from the sidelines. From Cindy, the oldest, who knew the game was up, to the youngest, Elliot's little girl, Kimmi. She wasn't quite two and seemed just as scared as Elliot said she had been with the mall Santa. Elliot never knew when enough was enough, because after she started crying on Santa's lap, Elliot picked her up and thrust her into Krampus' arms.

"Here, take a pic with him!"

When Elliot let go of her, Krampus had a look of horror and panic on his face, but Kimmi abruptly stopped crying. With a teary little smile she put her arms around him, rubbing her cheek against his furry shoulder. She giggled and someone snapped a picture. Krampus flinched at the flash and hissed, "Take her."

I took her before he dropped her. Now the joke wasn't so funny. He clattered away, but just to hide, not gone. His satchel full of chains and secret books lay on the piano next to his birch switch. I passed Kimmi to Aunt Maddy and went after Krampus, but in the dining room, Elliot caught up with me and crowed, "Look who I found under the mistletoe!"

I smiled and let him kiss me for the camera, but after the picture was taken, he tried to slip me some tongue.

"Don't be gross!" I hated sounding twelve years old, back when I'd thought he was cool, but was still squicked by girl-boy stuff.

"I'm just teasing." He blushed and retreated to the front room.

In the kitchen, the wreckage of pots and pans was still strewn around, waiting for Gram to clean up, which she usually would at about midnight, after everyone else had gone home or gone to bed.

Krampus stood at the sink, swabbing at his chest and shoulder with a wet dish towel. When he saw me, he scowled and muttered, "Filthy little hands. Covered in dirt and sticky with peppermint. Foul creatures."

"Don't you have errands to run tonight? Hint hint. Bad children to punish?"

He waved me off in an annoyed way. "There are always bad children to punish. Do you think they can only be whipped tonight?"

"I did actually think that."

"Only a myth."

"Like you," I said.

"Do I look like a myth?" He tossed down the dish towel like a gauntlet.

"You do kind of."

"And you kissed him."

"Who?"

"The father of those foul little creatures," he said, showing a lot of white teeth in a grimace.

"You know, I was a foul little creature like that."

"Never."

"You know I was." Even while I was saying it, I stepped closer to him. Not really consciously, just drifting toward him.

"You are not now."

He ran his hand down my back, his claws making a sinuous rasping sound against my shirt.

"This kissing, what is it like?"

"It's warm and sort of wet. You know."

"Like you."

"Not that wet," I said.

Not even thinking about it, I went up on my tiptoes to kiss him. I couldn't remember if I'd ever kissed a guy with a real beard before, but definitely not a beard like that. A beard that was everywhere, brushing against my lips, my chin, my neck, all whispery soft and smelling like spices. I closed the distance and pressed my lips against his, but he hesitated, almost shy, so that I had to tease his mouth open. Once I did, once our tongues touched, he pressed me back against the counter and kissed me

43

the way I'd always thought it should be done. Like kissing was a stand in for fucking. Like he wanted to eat me up. My blood was pounding through my veins so fast I felt lightheaded.

We would have been doing a lot more than kissing if Gram had walked in even a minute later than she did.

"How very scandalous! I don't know if you're allowed to kiss Krampus," she said.

"I think there is no rule against this," he said. He was panting and trying to smooth his beard out.

Still laughing, Gram came toward us with her hand out.

"I'm sorry, we haven't really gotten to meet. I'm Moritza's grandma, Elinore. They call me Ellie."

After a moment's hesitation, he took her hand, bent over it very genteelly, and kissed it.

"How continental," I sneered.

"I missed your name altogether," Grandma said.

His eyes flicked to mine as he came up out of the bow. "I am Krampus."

"His name is Peter." I picked it out of the air, but as soon as I said it I thought of that particular part of his anatomy and blushed.

"It's nice to meet you, Peter. You've really added some excitement to our old humdrum Christmas."

"It's not humdrum," I said.

"Peter, why don't you grab a plate of food and go out and socialize." Grandma was already moving him toward the door to the dining room, trying to trap me in the kitchen to be quizzed.

After he was gone, she said, "Well, who is he?"

"Just some guy."

"Just some guy you brought to Christmas and kissed in my kitchen!"

"I'm sorry." I was. I had no idea why I'd kissed him.

"Don't be sorry. I'm happy if you have a guy you like well enough to bring here and kiss him. And goodness he's built, if that's not too dirty old lady of me."

"Gram! Are you checking him out?"

"Let's just say, I don't know a lot of men who could pull off a tight bodysuit like that."

"He is kind of hot, isn't he?" I wanted to feel like I wasn't the only pervert who thought goat-man was sexy. Forget "kind of" hot. He was a hot, buttered crumpet of wrong. So wrong.

"At least now I know where you got that pine smell. I thought that was your perfume, but you've been smooching on him before tonight. Where did you meet him?"

"Just around."

"Just around? In Bavaria? What happened to Greg?" Grandma said.

"I don't know. He … I don't know what happened to him."

"Did you break up?"

"Yeah, but I don't want to talk about that tonight," I said.

"I just worry about you. It seems like you never have the kind of guy you really deserve. First with Scott and then–"

She was going to make me talk about it, but we were interrupted by the distinct sound of someone yowling in pain,

45

then yelling, laughter, and a sound I was learning to recognize: birches whistling through the air and making contact with someone's ass. I ran out of the kitchen and Gram came after me.

In the front room, my cousin Deborah had showed up with her son, Lance, who was a total shithead at age eleven. Krampus clearly had him pegged. The three of them were at a standoff. Krampus with his birches in hand, Lance clutching his backside, and Deborah standing between them yelling.

"I do not approve of corporal punishment!" she shouted.

"Aw, come on! Give him another whacking," Elliot said.

"Please, Mom, please can we go?" Lance was crying.

"Where do you get off hitting my child? You don't hit other people's kids. Especially not as a joke," Deborah said.

Shaking the birches, Krampus showed her his teeth. "A joke? Do you find it amusing that he steals money from you? Do you laugh to know that he breaks windows, dumps rubbish bins, and pushes down little children who are soft in the head?"

There was a moment of stunned silence. Lance's eyes got wide and nervous, and although Deborah said, "He does no such thing," I could see her thinking.

Then Elliot laughed, and so did everyone else, except Deborah and Lance.

"That's not funny," Deborah said. "I don't care what kind costume he's wearing, I don't like this game."

Krampus made her a little bow, saying, "I apologize, *mein Frau*."

When he put the birches back on the top of the piano, I saw the look he gave Lance, who was still cowering behind his mother. It was a look that said, "You and I will finish our business later."

Everyone else played it down, with Elliot telling Lance not to be such a crybaby. Then Deborah took Lance into the kitchen, and Krampus sat back down with his plate of food.

"Children are amoral." He used a claw to skewer a piece of ham and tuck it into his mouth. He chewed it lovingly and then said, "If they are not taught good from bad, they grow into immoral adults."

"I still don't think corporal punishment works," Aunt Sheila said.

"Spare the rod, spoil the child," Krampus intoned to a scoop of whipped sweet potatoes. He licked them off his fingers with a smile.

"That's right," Uncle Dean said. "That's in the Bible."

"Besides, that little twerp deserves a whipping," Elliot said.

"You are Elliot Marchand, yes?" Krampus said.

"Yeah. I'm Moritza's cousin."

"The one who burned down the little hut that once stood in the garden."

"Huh, what?" Elliot said. His head jerked around, looking at everyone in the room. Gram looked back with a frown.

"When you were a little boy. Grandmama said no firecrackers for you. And you were angry and so you wanted to make a fire–"

"What are you talking about?" Elliot wore a nervous grin now.

"The shed in the back yard," Gram said. "It burned down, I guess it would have been the summer you were eight. I always wondered how it got started. I figured it was some neighborhood kids."

"Well, it wasn't me!" Elliot said.

Krampus took another bite of food, nodding to himself.

"And so you took the box of matches out of the drawer in the kitchen and you made a fire. Only it got much bigger than you expected, the way fires will."

"Moritza, did you set him up to do this?" Gram said.

"Almost had you going, didn't he?" I forced out a laugh and Gram joined me. Elliot didn't. He looked pale and sweaty.

Since Krampus wasn't looking at me, I nudged him in the leg. To tell him to stop. After a moment he shifted his gaze from Elliot and winked at me. Setting his plate of food next to a glass of iced tea on a side table, he patted his hairy knee. I went. For the same reason I'd kissed him, I suppose. I should have been repulsed by him, but instead I felt this steady itching attraction.

"I do think someone needs to take that Lance to hand. Debbie sure can't handle him," Uncle Dean said.

"He got suspended again. That's the third time this year," said Aunt Sheila.

I intended to just balance on Krampus' knees, but he eased me backward until I was leaning against him, square in his lap. His completely unclothed lap. Within a few minutes, he'd let his part in the conversation lapse and sat quietly with an arm around my waist. There was a steady feed of electricity between us and then it surged with a faintly audible pop.

His breath got quicker and shallower against my neck. The smell of Christmas got stronger. Then unmistakably I felt something press into my back. It grew from a small hard knot to a heavy throbbing rod. And when he started to sneak up the hem of my shirt, I let him, until his cock was rubbing against my bare back. It felt as hot and damp as it had looked the night before.

I leaned back and whispered, "If you were wearing some pants, we could get up and go into my bedroom."

He grunted.

I rocked against him and when that made him squirm, I said, "This shirt is so itchy." I reached back like I was going to scratch myself, but pressed my hand to small of my back and ran my palm up his cock.

"Mercy," he whimpered.

I was having fun messing with him, when Aunt Maddy stood up and reminded us we weren't alone.

"I think I'm going to head home, but I want my picture taken with Krampus," she said.

I shifted in his lap and he made a panicked noise in response. He'd asked for mercy, so I gave it to him. I reached for his empty plate and half-full iced tea glass, like I meant to clear them away. As I stood up, though, I emptied the glass into his lap. An effective but unpleasant solution, based on the sound he made.

"Oh shit! I'm sorry. Sorry! I hope I didn't ruin your fur."

"You don't hear that very often." Aunt Sheila laughed.

I dabbed at him with a napkin, but he pushed my hand away and stood up.

"Sorry! Let me show you where the bathroom is. See if we can get your costume dry."

In the bathroom, he glared at me while he dabbed his wet crotch with a towel.

"See? Clothes would be helpful in a situation like that. I wouldn't have had to dump iced tea on you."

"It is your fault. It does that because of you," he said. "It never grows so big when I ..."

"When you what? When you fool around with the elves?"

I backed off that joke when he snarled. His tail flicked angrily against me.

"When I ... pleasure myself." He coughed and lifted his chin in a very dignified way.

"Seriously? When you do it yourself, you don't get a hard on like that?"

"Is that what you call it? A hard on?"

"Well, yeah, or an erection."

He lost his dignified look and snorted. "I want to erect it again."

He tossed the towel onto the edge of the tub and grabbed me. I made a half-hearted effort to get away, mostly for the pleasure of letting him prove he was bigger and stronger than me. It definitely wasn't that I wanted to get away, because as soon as he'd subdued me, I kissed him like crazy. His tongue was

50

madness. There was so much of it and it was like a living creature with a mind of its own. His hands were that way, too, slipping around my bra to my breasts. Just like that, his cock eased out of its sheath and jabbed me in the belly. The iced tea was forgiven.

I pushed him back a step until he was against the bathroom door, because by then I wanted to return the favor. Last night, I hadn't been entirely sure, but at that moment, I went down on my knees without hesitation.

He tasted like stollen. Like marzipan and candied fruit.

Okay, not really, but I wouldn't have been surprised if he had. No, he tasted like salt and flesh with a hint of orange. The sound he made when I slid his cock as far into my mouth as it would comfortably go, that sound was immediate payoff. It was the sound of somebody who'd just discovered the most amazing thing in the world. He'd just discovered water. Air. Gravity. Flying. His head knocked back against the door and his knees went wobbly.

He was a few degrees shy of too hot, and slippery all on his own. That was nice, not having to be the only one supplying the lubrication. My lips slid effortlessly down the shaft and back up, but the surprise was that it wasn't perfectly smooth. He didn't have just a single ridge around the crown. He had a series of ridges descending below the crown on the underside of his cock. Like little speed bumps, rumbling against my lower lip until it tingled.

Doggy style. He was built for doggy style. Just the thought made me squirm and press my thighs together. Shouldn't even think about that. Dangerous to think about that. I sucked harder, ran my tongue along that line of ridges, until he was gasping. With one hand, I made a little exploration into his fur, combing it with my fingers until I found his balls. Too hairy to suck by a long shot, but when I petted them, he made a sound like *mhmmm*. With my other hand, I helped things along by stroking his shaft.

I'd completely soaked my panties and I thought things were going pretty well when he said, "Wait, wait. You don't want such _"

"It's okay. I know how it works," I mumbled around his cock.

"No, no. Wait."

It was a minor tug of war, with me trying to keep his cock in my mouth and him trying to pull it out. The reverse of how things like that usually went, and that turned out to be pretty hot. He cupped my face in hands and tried to push me back, but I put my hands on his hips and pulled him deeper into my mouth.

"*Bitte*," he moaned, and then a few seconds later, "*Nein. Watte.*"

He pushed at me harder, so I opened my mouth to let his cock slip out. He gasped. His semen hit me square in the cheek and splattered up into my hair and into his fur.

"*Scheisse!*" he said. He stayed on his feet – his hooves, but his legs were shaking. When I stood up, trying to catch a drip running off my chin, he looked stunned.

"It's okay, see?

"It is?" He reached out and wiped at my cheek.

"Now, it's all even. You did a nice thing for me and I did a nice thing for you."

He frowned, but didn't say anything.

"Well, we made another mess trying to clean up the first one." I tossed him the towel he'd been drying himself with, so he could clean up.

"Hey," Aunt Maddy called from the hallway. "I need to get out of here. You almost done?"

"Sure! Just a sec." I washed my hands and face, checked my hair, and reached for the door, but Krampus was still standing there. He held the towel in one hand, but he hadn't moved. I took the towel and wiped him down. I'd meant to be all business-like about it, but I might have spent more time than was strictly necessary, marveling at the muscles under his fur. His thighs were massive and taut, and I could have bounced quarters off his belly. Realizing that I was just petting him now, I gave him one final smoothing over and decided he didn't look too suspect.

He still hadn't said anything, but when I reached past him and opened the door, he went out to the front room and dutifully had his picture taken with Aunt Maddy, and then with Aunt Sheila and Uncle Dean. After they left, the party started to dwindle down, and by eleven o'clock, everyone who was going home had left. Then it was just Elliot and his girls, and a few other cousins who planned to stay.

We were discussing the configurations of who would sleep where, when Krampus shouldered his satchel and picked up his birches.

53

"Oh, you're not staying?" Grandma said.

"*Danke, mein Frau*, but no. A busy night for me."

She came across the room to hug him, like he was some boyfriend I'd brought for Christmas. "We're glad you came, Peter. I hope you'll come back and let us meet you some time when you're not in costume."

He smiled at her and then stepped out onto the porch.

I went after him and tugged on his satchel to turn him around. Separated by a stair tread, we were nearly eye to eye, but even though I was right there, he didn't do anything. So I kissed him. Big deal. Gram already thought he was a boyfriend, so I could get away with kissing him on the porch. He didn't do anything, which made me think I'd messed it up. I wasn't sure how, but that was so typical of me. Maybe he thought I was a slut, the way I'd gone down on my knees in the bathroom. When I pulled away, though, he jerked me back and kissed me. While one hand crept up under my shirt, the other slid down to my ass.

He stepped down so that I was over him, and put both hands up my shirt to wrestle with my bra. "Ah, you keep them caged," he muttered.

He wrestled with my bra for a few moments and then gave up. Releasing me, he hopped down to the bottom of the steps.

"You're really going?"

"As you say, I have much work to do tonight."

Oh now, now he was going to pull that out. When I'd been counting on him staying the night. When I'd spent the last hour thinking about how to squeeze him into my twin bed. I'd evened up the score by sucking him off and now I wanted to make the score uneven again.

Instead, I spent the night alone in my bed, with Elliot's little girls sleeping on an air mattress on the floor. Long after Tiffany and Kimmi were asleep, I was awake, tossing and turning, aroused and confused. I had no idea what Krampus was, but I wanted him.

I worried that I'd put him off. Turned him off. I worried that after he got his trinket back, that would be it. And after all, what was the alternative? Whatever he was, he didn't exactly fit into everyday life. I fell asleep thinking those pragmatic thoughts.

Chapter Four

All I Want For Christmas Is *Mein Schmuckstück*

I woke to the sound of my cousins going crazy over their toys. When I shuffled out to the kitchen Gram hugged me hard and said, "You're awfully sly."

"What does that mean?"

"Well, I know I didn't buy oranges to put in the kids' Christmas stockings."

There they were: big, fat, delicious smelling oranges, bulging out the toes of all the socks hanging from the mantel. Krampus.

When I was little, Christmas seemed to go by in a flash. A rush of toys, candy, lights, snow, and then BOOM! You were sitting at your desk in Mrs. Collier's classroom, still hung-over from the sugar high and excitement, staring down five more months of school.

As an adult, with a secret and a mission, Christmas crawled by for me. The kids went back and forth all morning. To the tree to open another present, then into the kitchen to stuff fresh cinnamon rolls into their mouths, then back to the tree. They decimated the wrapped packages, ravaged their stockings, and careered around the house like maniacs. That was all before 8:30. I took a slower approach, opening a sweater from Gram, some bubble bath and lotion from Elliot and the girls, and then bypassing the handful of little gag gifts to work the orange out of the toe of my stocking.

It was, without exaggeration, the most amazing orange I had ever tasted. Sweet, tart, juicy. Magical. I ate all of mine and then began to scavenge around for anyone who hadn't already eaten theirs. That's how I knew they were magical oranges, though. Everyone was already tearing theirs open and eating them. Even Tiffany, who usually acted like fruits and vegetables were poisonous, was clamoring for her dad to help her get the peel off.

Then there was the agony of helping Gram get ready for lunch, with her dropping hints, trying to get me to talk about "Peter" or tell her about my break-up with Greg. I'd been putting that topic off for months. Then I had to get through the actual lunch, with another horde of relatives crammed into the house, and all the usual questions about when was I graduating, when was I getting married, when was I having kids. My whole life on fast forward. A couple of people started hinting around about "the Holenkranz money," but Gram shut that down with a few well-placed glares.

It went on and on and on, until finally, the madness stopped. Or anyway, the madness took a nap. Between all the excitement and the food, people started crashing out left and right. By three o'clock, every bed, couch, recliner, and empty corner in the house was full of nappers. Two minutes after that I was rifling through the phone book in the kitchen. Vandy Harris' house was only seven blocks away. Walking distance on a crisp winter day.

That's how crazy the whole situation with Krampus and Bettina was making me. I was seriously just going to stroll over to Vandy Harris' house, on Christmas Day, mind you, and say what? *Oh hai, I just dropped by to see if you stole my grandmother's vacuum after accidentally sucking up a reindeer bead that belongs to Santa Claus' sidekick*. Insane. I did it anyway. Put on my coat and scarf, and struck out in the snow toward Thistle Street.

I turned over in my mind how to broach the subject as I walked along, kicking up plumes of snow. The truth was too goofy. Even if Krampus wasn't a hallucination, and I had definitely not gone down on a hallucination in Gram's bathroom, he was not Real. Not in the way the stuff you see every day is Real. So it had to be simple: *I dropped something on the rug in Bettina's room. I think you may have accidentally vacuumed it up*. Neutral. Non-accusatory. I would even say something like, "When you go into work after the holiday, could you check the vacuum for me?" So it wouldn't seem like I even suspected her of stealing a vacuum.

I felt like I'd perfected my plan when I reached Vandy's house and realized she wasn't home. Wasn't home and wasn't coming home. Nobody had even shoveled the drive or the sidewalk. Some small part of me hoped that she had robbed the old bitch blind and skipped town. Except for the part where everything that had once belonged to the old bitch was now mine, and I didn't want to be robbed blind.

The reality was that Vandy hadn't skipped town with a bunch of stolen property. Vandy had gone out of town for Christmas, and there I stood in front of her house like an idiot. I did what any self-respecting newly rich slut would do. I tried the garage door and found it unlocked. Glancing up and down the street, I saw a beige sedan with its engine running, but it was halfway down the block and facing the other direction. Not likely to see me. I hoisted the garage door open, like I belonged there and had every right to do it. Inside was proof of what I'd always suspected: Vandy Harris was a clean freak. Her garage was immaculate. Instead of being crammed to the rafters with recycling and every random piece of crap furniture and cardboard box of Christmas decorations, her garage was empty. A few shelves of tools and paint cans. A freezer. A ladder. A big empty space where she probably stored – gasp! – her car. I hear some people actually use their garages for that.

I'd already basically broken into her house, so I plunged ahead. She may have been a neat freak, but she wasn't very security conscious. The door from the garage to the house was unlocked, so I walked right in.

There was a Christmas tree in one corner of the living room, but that was the only thing I would have described as clutter. Everything else looked like it was a model home. Still, I wasn't there to admire her décor or her housekeeping habits, so I went straight for the closets. The nice thing was that her house was basically a mirror of Gram's. All those little post-war ranches built on the same three or four sets of blueprints. The bedroom

closets, I discounted out of hand. The coat closet was where
Gram kept her vacuum, but Vandy's had nothing but neatly hung
coats and rows of shoes. The linen closet was as advertised.
Perfectly folded and stacked sheets, towels, and blankets. I was
stumped until I remembered the pantry. Gram's had long since
been turned into a mudroom/junk room/catchall.

Vandy's was still a pantry and, neatly arrayed opposite
canned goods, stood her cleaning supplies. I recognized the
vacuum immediately as a foreign object. Not that I had ever seen
it in Bettina's house, but that it clearly didn't belong in Vandy's
house. It was one of those fancy, cyclonic, orgasmic, life-
changing vacuums with triple filtration and something something
bagless *wunderbar*. I guessed it was at least a thousand-dollar
vacuum, because that was the sort of thing Bettina would buy for
her housekeeper to use.

I wheeled the vacuum out into the kitchen to have better light,
but it was less the lack of light that was a problem, and more my
lack of familiarity with the machine. The only vacuum I'd ever
used was Gram's ancient Hoover with a dusty bag. This thing
didn't even have a bag. I could see the tube where the dirt went,
but I couldn't figure out how to get it open.

I'd left the garage door open so as not to attract too much
attention. That was why I didn't hear Vandy coming home. She
simply pulled into the open garage and walked in through the
kitchen door to find me wrestling with the vacuum on her kitchen
floor.

She gave the kind of scream that people in movies give when a velociraptor has just bitten their asses off. When she finished screaming, she said, "Oh god. Oh god. Moritza. Please don't call the police."

Wasn't that supposed to be my line? Hadn't I broken into her house?

"Look, Vandy. I can explain, okay?"

"Oh god." She put her hands over her mouth, but she kept saying, "Oh god."

She went to high school with my mother. I tried to imagine my mother at that age, looking like that. Vandy was going gray and a good fifty pounds overweight, while my mother was frozen for all time at a slender, smiling twenty-six. It made me sad.

"The thing is, I dropped something really important on my grandmother's bedroom floor, and when I went back yesterday to look for it, I saw that you'd vacuumed. Only I couldn't find the vacuum and so I was going to come here and ask you—"

"I'm not a bad person!" Vandy blurted. "I just. I don't know why I did it. Please don't call the police. I can take it back. I'll return it. I'll—"

"No, it's okay. I just need to see if the thing I lost is in the vacuum. I checked the other vacuums at the house. I was going to ask you, but then you weren't here, and the door wasn't locked. I'm really sorry."

"You won't call the police? I'll take the vacuum back. And the Lladro Christmas angel. I'm not a bad person."

"No, it's fine. Keep the vacuum. And the angel. Just help me get it–"

"You really won't call the police? I'll take it all back, the vacuum, the Christmas angel, that cashmere throw."

"Jesus, Vandy, did you clear the place out?" I said. I was mostly joking, but she burst into tears.

"I'm so sorry. But you don't know. You don't know how horrible she was to me."

"Actually, I do, Vandy. I do know how horrible she was to you. I'm sorry. Look, I'm not going to call the police. You can keep whatever you took. I don't care. I just need to find this bead I dropped. I really need it. Please, can you help?"

Vandy nodded, smudging her face with her tears.

"I can open it, but the bead's not in there. I emptied out the dirt from Mrs. von Holenkranz' house. It's in the trash up at the house."

I believed her, but I still let her open up the vacuum and go through the dirt in it. There was no bead. If it had ever been in that vacuum, it was still up at the house.

"I'll go up to the house right now and look," she blubbered.

"No, it's okay. I was going up there anyway. You stay home. It's Christmas. Enjoy the rest of your Christmas."

I was going to slip out the same way I'd come in, but she was standing between me and the door. She looked so sad and so scared that I hugged her. For a moment she sagged against me, snuffling in my ear, and then she stepped back and let me go.

As I was almost to the end of the block, the door of the beige sedan opened and a man in a Santa suit stepped out.

"Ho ho ho! Merrrrryyyyy Christmas!" he chortled. Warming up, I guess.

"Yeah. Merry Christmas," I said. I didn't smile or look at him. I walked away as fast as I could, not worried anymore that he might have seen me go into Vandy's house, but feeling that familiar Santa queasiness in my stomach.

I walked back to Gram's house, more hopeful about finding the bead, but a lot more tired. Seeing what Bettina did to everyone around her always had that effect on me.

Chapter Five

Away In A Manger

"You're going out again? It's Christmas," Gram said, when I told her I was going up to Bettina's before dinner.

"I know, but I want to take care of a few things." I was already wrestling back into my coat and I could smell Krampus on me, like he was standing right beside me.

"I thought everything was ready for the funeral."

"It is. There are just a couple of things I need to take care of."

"Do you need some help?"

"No, everything's fine." Well-intentioned "help" was the last thing I needed.

I drove up to Bettina's house – my house – and started in on the trash cans, digging for the contents of the vacuum. I found the collection of dust and lint that had surely come out of the vacuum, but there was no bead. Then I repeated the humiliating trek to Bettina's room, then down the hall, up the stairs, and to my room, crawling the entire way, looking for Krampus' trinket. It wasn't there.

I ended the journey, lying on the floor of my childhood bedroom, staring up at Snowy. He seemed, as always, on the

verge of frenetic movement. His head cocked curiously, his front
paws drawn up, his tail coiled behind him. Ready for action. That
was quality taxidermy. Only the best for Bettina von Holenkranz.

"What is it, Snowy? What's the matter? Did Timmy fall down
the well?" I said.

He didn't answer. He never did.

I knew I should get up and go. Gram would be wondering
what had happened to me. It was past dinner time. I felt
overwhelmed, though. Not by Krampus' missing trinket, but by
the enormity of being an heiress. It always looked so easy on
reality TV, but I knew there were still a ton of things to sort out. I
felt tired just thinking about it.

After lying there a little longer, I dragged myself up and went
back to Gram's house.

At least the Official Holiday was winding down. The lunch
crowd had dispersed after their naps, and few of them returned
for dinner leftovers. The cookies and candies were decimated,
and the wrapping paper already bundled into the recycling bin.

I still felt grimy from digging through trash and crawling
around on the floor, so I took a shower, and ate dinner in my
flannel nightgown.

"You look tired," Gram said. "Why don't you go to bed?"

I wasn't as tired as I was worried, but I took her offer. I dug
around in her medicine cabinet looking for something to help me
sleep, but the heaviest thing she had was a nighttime pain killer. I
took one with a swig of water out of the faucet and shuffled off to
my bedroom.

My bedroom. My quiet idyll, where I had been safe from the torments of adolescence.

Krampus lay on my bed, one leg crossed over the other, while his hands were stretched overhead to hold up the *Cosmo* magazine he was reading.

He'd cluttered up the floor beside the bed with his satchel, chains, birch twigs, and a few oranges that had spilled out of his bag. I closed the door quickly, in case anyone was coming down the hallway.

"What are you doing here?" I hissed.

"Waiting for you."

"Well, I didn't find your trinket. I don't know where it is."

"This we will worry about tomorrow," he said.

He laid the magazine down and stood up to consider me in my frumpy nightgown. I waited for him to leave, but he didn't.

"I'm going to sleep. Turn out the light when you go."

Except he didn't go. After I got into bed, he turned off the lamp and crawled into bed with me. Between the sheets it was so cold, I wanted to get up and tell Gram to turn the thermostat up from 64 degrees. Soon enough, I would have the money to make sure she didn't have to freeze during the winter.

"You need to go," I said. "If my grandmother finds you in here–"

"She will compliment me on my costume, yes? She will say, 'Oh, Peter, do you want something to eat?' And I would not refuse more ham."

"Okay, fine, yes, she probably would. You still need to go. Don't you have work to do?"

"I do not work every moment of the day. I must sleep also."

He snuggled closer. Even though his hooves were two cold little intruders near my feet, the rest of him was so warm, like being bundled in a heated fur blanket. Plus he made all those nice man sounds. Little grunts of satisfaction and sleepiness, while he nuzzled against my neck and hair.

Something soft swept around my ankles and calves. His tail. I scooched my lower half a bit further from him, but he pursued, pressing himself against my back.

"Mmmm," he said into my ear.

"What's your name, really?"

"Krampus."

"That's not a real name, though," I said.

He brought his left hand to rest on my waist, rubbing my side. Then his hand crept over to my belly and began to pet that. The slutty part of me wanted to roll over like a puppy and open my legs. Yes, pet my belly.

"I was also called Klaubauf and Bartl and Pelzebock."

"Pelzebock? Those are all awful."

"Zwarte Piet, too, which means Black Peter."

"Then you are named Peter?" I laughed in surprise. It pleased me that I had randomly picked a name that was actually his.

"After a fashion." His tail was back, making long, languorous forays around my ankles, my calves, and then trying to sneak up under my night gown. At first I clamped my knees together, but a

68

tail isn't as easy to thwart as a roaming hand. The tail slithered up the back of my nightgown and brushed against my butt. It reminded me of this big powder puff Bettina had owned when I was little. I was allowed to dust myself all over with powder after I took a bath. The puff had been so luxuriant, brushing over my bare skin.

That silky whisking tail weakened my resolve. And the muscles that held my knees closed. As soon as I stopped resisting, Peter's tail found its way to the front of my nightgown, where it proceeded to brush teasingly all up the fronts of my thighs and then stroke gently at my pubic hair. His hand all the while was working up from my belly to my breasts. It didn't take him very long to find my left nipple, which he circled over and over with the tip of his finger and then his claw. I didn't help him, but I didn't stop him as he teased the buttons of my nightgown open until he reached bare skin, where he repeated the circuit around my nipple.

It stood up eagerly and the right one joined it.

Now that he had my nightgown open, he cupped my breast in his hand. His palms and the pads of his fingers were calloused, as rough as you'd expect from someone whose job involved wielding a bundle of birches. It was a delicious contrast to that soft tail.

I stayed on my side, turned away from him, but all he had to do was lean over me and unfurl that tongue to reach my nipples. It circled around, hot and wet, then drew into a sinuous noose, drawing my nipple tighter. I couldn't help myself. I let a moan out, and he answered it, pressing his hips against my backside so I could feel how his cock was growing.

Trouble, pure trouble. I had to be crazy to keep doing this.

"Well, if you don't have sex with elves, who do you have sex with? Because there's no way I'm the first." I figured that might be the best way to extricate myself. Get the topic onto other women. I've never been able to stand hearing a guy talk about his other conquests.

"The first human, yes." Now that he had my nipples under the power of his tongue, his hand traipsed back down my belly toward his other goal.

"Then who?"

"Oh, fauns mostly. They are not so smart, but they will lift their tails for anyone. There was a selkie once. She smelled horribly of fish. And she was always cold and damp. And two pixies, who are dirty creatures. Not as bad as elves, but nasty all the same."

"Two of them? At the same time?"

"Mmmm," Peter murmured and teased my nipple between his sharp teeth.

"You had a threesome with pixies. Of course."

He didn't bother to answer. He was too busy working on getting my nightgown off.

"And you didn't kiss them?"

"Kissing is a thing that humans do," he said. His big rough palm was petting my thighs now. I put my hand on top of his and made him stop.

"Look, I really can't tonight," I said. "I need to sleep. I have a funeral to go to tomorrow."

He ignored that. I elbowed him hard in the gut. Hard enough to make him fall off my very narrow bed onto the floor. He let out a bleat of laughter.

"Moritza? You okay in there?" Gram called.

She was drinking and playing cards with some friends, including Digger. I was starting to suspect he might be her boyfriend, so the last thing I wanted to do was ruin her night.

"Fine, Gram. Just clumsy."

Peter stretched his legs up to the bed and danced a jig against my ass with his hooves.

I jumped out of bed and snapped on the light. He lay on the floor, his hooves still propped against the bed. There I was trying to straighten my nightgown, while he sprawled out on my floor, wearing nothing but a grin and a throbbing erection.

"You have to go. You should go. I'm sorry I haven't found your bead. I'm sorry my grandmother ruined your life, too. I'm sorry, but–"

"Ch-ch, Moritza. No. There is no ruining."

His tail caressed my leg, tickling and comforting at once.

I meant to step over him, to go out to the bathroom to get, to get a tissue, or a drink, or just some fresh air. I needed to clear my head. That's what I was going to do. Absolutely.

Except when I stepped over him, he caught my ankle in one hand and the hem of my nightgown in the other.

"Yes, I will go, *kleine* Moritza. Only let me have another taste of you, first."

His hand crept up and up my leg, while the other tugged at my nightgown, pulling me down. When I made a show of resistance, his claws dug into my leg to discourage me. It made me shiver, half with excitement, half with fear. There I was again, doing a dance with a wild animal. A show of resistance was all I had, because there was something so alluring about engulfing him under my nightgown, as I slowly lowered myself to his mouth.

That tongue.

That tongue.

There was no tentative exploration this time. As soon as I was in reach, he used his tongue to draw elaborate patterns all along my labia, before the tip of his tongue flicked against my clit.

It was some sort of crazy yoga pose, with his hooves still propped on the bed, and me squatting over him, arching my back over his knees to rest my hands on the bed. I knew I would be sorry later, with all kinds of mysterious aches and pains, but I just didn't care. I arched my back more, to present my pussy to him more fully. I wanted to be fucked, and no exaggeration, his tongue was more amazing than any of the cocks I'd encountered in my short life. It slid into me, first slow and teasing, then quick and urgent, always returning to lash my clit like he was wielding a birch bundle.

My back was starting to hurt and I worried that I wouldn't be able to keep the noise down. When I stood up, he cursed at me.

"*Nein*, come back here!" he said.

"Shh!"

"Shh? I will make such a ruckus if you don't come back here."

Standing there, feeling wobbly, I saw the perfect solution: his cock.

I peeled out of my nightgown, turned around knelt again. I delivered myself up to his insane tongue again, but this time with something to keep me quiet.

Up until then, fellatio had always seemed like such a mechanical process. I mostly focused on doing it right, and didn't much focus on enjoying it. Going down on Krampus changed that. It took me right back to the childhood pleasure of slurping on a popsicle. A hot, orange popsicle. Gawd, I felt so slutty, but it was wonderful. I drew him in as far as I could and applied just enough suction to make it slow work getting him out. After the first few moments, I wasn't even thinking anymore. I matched his pace, slower or faster, and the closer I got to my orgasm, the deeper I took him.

By then he had one arm around my waist and with the other hand he dug his claws into my rump. When I came, I didn't even care if he was in danger of drowning. Moaning around his cock, I bore down and thrust against his tongue. He answered me with a sudden bucking of his hips and a mouthful of semen that left a strange tingling sensation at the back of my throat.

I had no idea whether we'd managed to be quiet enough, but we were both so spent, we just collapsed on the floor and snuggled against each other. I think I could have fallen asleep right there, except that just as I was fading out, he bit me on the ass.

"I suppose you want to whip me for being a 'bad girl,'" I said.

"*Nein.* Whipping is only for children. I do not want to whip this ass."

He did want to keep biting it, though, and his teeth were sharp. When I stood up and reached for my nightgown, he said, "No, I'll be good."

"When people say that to you, do you ever believe them?"

"No, but children are little lying liars."

"And you're not?"

"On my honor," he purred, but he ruined the sincerity of the moment by flicking his tongue at me.

All the same, I left the nightgown off and let him get back into bed with me. I imagined that's what it felt like to turn a mink coat inside out. To be wrapped up in sumptuous fur as you drift off to sleep.

"Peter?" I wanted to test the waters of that. Of calling him by a normal name.

"*Ja?*" he said.

"So you really don't live at the North Pole?"

"Always with that question. No. Why would I live at the North Pole?"

"I don't know. I guess because you and Santa Claus are buddies? I just figured you lived in the same place. Next door to each other."

"What is this 'bud-eez'?"

"Friends," I said.

He made an annoyed grumbling noise and raised himself up on an elbow to look at me.

"Herr Klaus is no friend of mine. If he were my friend, would he not have helped me? For all these years, he has known about the charm and yet he did nothing. Perhaps your grandmother did not need to steal a thread from his coat. Perhaps he gave it to her himself. No, we are not friends. I think he was pleased to have me gone. To see me made powerless."

"Oh." For a while that was all I could think of to say. Then I added, "I never liked Santa Claus anyway."

That made him laugh.

"Well, if you don't live at the North Pole, where do you live then?" I said.

"Come."

He pushed back the covers and got out of bed. Taking my hand he pulled me up, too. I didn't know what he was doing, but he led me across my bedroom to the door. When he reached for the doorknob, I said, "No! Hang on! I'm not dressed."

"Hush. Come quietly."

I was still trying to pull my hand out of his when he swung my bedroom door open.

On the other side wasn't the hallway of my grandma's house. On the other side was a dark, dense forest lying under a coverlet of snow. Krampus tugged on my hand again and I followed, utterly naked, hypnotized by the sight.

The snow was cold under my feet and the night air swirled around me, making me shiver. Snowflakes kissed my arms and shoulders, melting as soon as they touched. I was about to complain about the cold and my nakedness, when I saw where he was leading me, just a few more steps through that snow globe of a forest. In the center of a clearing, where the whole Milky Way winked down at us, stood a stone cottage. When we reached it, he opened the door and gestured an expansive welcome to his home.

Inside, the cottage was dark and cold until Krampus dragged his claw along the edge of the fireplace. Sparks leapt from the stone, and across the room, a pair of candles lit in a wall sconce. An instant later, fire flared up in the hearth. In the real world, even if you could start a fire that quickly, it would take hours for a stone cottage in a wintry forest to warm up. That was how I knew it wasn't the real world. As soon as the fire was lit, the cottage's single room was warm enough that I stopped shivering in my bare skin.

In front of the fireplace stood a plain wooden table and a single chair. In the corner was a cupboard, which I doubted contained any clothes. The only other piece of furniture was a bed. Still leading me by the hand, he drew back the curtains around the bed. Even there, where the drapes would have kept out the heat, the air was warm and gentle. The bed was made up with silks and heavy furs that enveloped me when I crawled into them. He slid into the covers beside me and then I had a means of comparison. Peter was in fact softer than the furs.

Chapter Six

O Come, All Ye Faithful

I woke up from the most pleasant dream. I was bundled up, warm even as snowflakes fell on my cheeks. Strong arms carried me through a cold night with the moon hanging overhead. My head rested on a man's shoulder as he carried me. My father, I thought. Sometimes I was sure I remembered him carrying me when I was little.

As I rolled over in bed, something soft trapped my legs. I lifted up the sheets and found myself wrapped up in a black silk robe I'd never seen before. So it hadn't been a dream, and it hadn't been my father carrying me. Peter had carried me back from his cottage through the woods to my grandmother's house.

I lay in bed, drifting in and out of sleep, trying to sort out what might be real, what might have been a dream. The cottage? The fur-covered bed? I didn't remember putting on the robe, so he must have wrapped it around me. He'd left it behind. That and the ghost of his scent.

When Gram came in later to wake me up, she sniffed the room and sat down on the edge of the bed. I pulled the covers up to my chin, so she maybe wouldn't notice I was wearing something other than what I'd gone to bed in. Then she picked my nightgown up off the floor and laid it across the bed. Oops.

"I'll have you know that young man of yours came out of here last night wearing a mile-wide grin," she said. She was grinning pretty widely herself.

"He what?"

"Oh, you thought he was going to keep this a little secret?"

"I didn't–"

"Or you thought your old Gram was too doddy to figure things out?"

"Well, I'm sorry. I hope he didn't wake you up or anything."

Gram laughed. "Wake me up? We were still playing poker! Digger's a regular night owl. Peter sat down and played cards with us until the sun came up. Drank up my good Scotch. And that boy can talk. He's like something out of *The Canterbury Tales*. He knows some very old and unbelievably filthy stories. And the most hilarious rants about elves. Is that what he studies? Folklore?"

"Oh my god," I whispered. He'd hung out and drunk with my grandma?

"He may be swarthy as all get out, but he is definitely Bavarian. Through and through."

"Swarthy?" Was that a polite way of saying black and hairy? "And what kind of dirty stories?"

"Don't look so horrified. He's a charming young man, if a bit … odd."

Odd. That was the simplest thing you could say about him, but to my amazement, that was all Gram had to say about him. Of course, it was still Christmas when she saw him, so I suppose the costume lie could hold some water. Today, though, and tomorrow? And every other day of the year, excepting Halloween and New Year's? He couldn't keep coming around looking the way he did.

I should have been relieved to know that his days of being able to pop in and have a drink with Gram were limited, but it made me sad, too. The whole day was like that. A trip to the funeral parlor to drop off Bettina's clothes. Then to the newspaper to make sure the obituary was right. Enough truth not to seem smarmy, but enough lies that Bettina wouldn't be immortalized as the raging bitch she was. After that, I went by the church to promise Father Dalton that he'd get a nice donation for agreeing to have the funeral there. He'd been burned enough times by Bettina that he was understandably nervous. And it wasn't that I was belatedly grieving Bettina, it was that the process of preparing for a funeral is sad no matter whose funeral it is. Funerals make you think too much about your own life. Where it's going. Where it's not going.

I went back to Gram's house drained and more than half-hoping that Peter would be lounging on my bed when I got there. He wasn't. I suppose he understood that his window of public appearances was small. I imagined that was why he'd had so few chances to socialize with human females. Aside from the disgusting little ones.

Lying alone in my bed, things started to settle around me. The knowledge that I was a semester away from finishing my graduate degree and I didn't have any plans. I'd gone to grad school, because I didn't know what else to do. When I finished grad school, what then?

That logy, doomy feeling carried all the way through to the morning. I got up earlier than I had to and Gram made us breakfast. I hoped we'd eat in quiet, but after she'd stirred her coffee full of sugar, she said, "So what happens now?"

I almost cried, but I kept it all buttoned up and smiled and said, "Well, I need to get back to school."

"So soon." She frowned into her coffee mug. That was when I realized she'd been hoping I would stay. I didn't know how to answer that, so I stood up and leaned over to give her a hug. The kind of hug that keeps you from having to look at the other person.

"I have to get ready for the spring semester. Finish studying for my exams."

She nodded and took a drink of her coffee.

"I think I'll go ahead and get dressed. Make sure everything is ready. The limo from Grayson's should be here about ten-thirty. I'll just meet you at the church."

I needed to escape. Not from Gram, but from myself. I almost managed, stuffed into a brand new black dress and hose and heels, feeling like a stranger inside my body. I wouldn't have been surprised to wake up and find it was a dream, but no matter

how hard I pinched myself on the drive to the church, I didn't
wake up.

The funeral wasn't until eleven, but the church was unlocked
when I got there. In the foyer I called out, "Father Dalton," but no
one answered. Probably still at the rectory having breakfast.

I walked up the aisle, bypassing the font, and tried to think of
the last time I'd been there. Gram had never been very big on
going to church, and Grandpa Albert had told me that I could find
God anywhere I looked. When I was little I'd gone through
confirmation, and we usually went for the big holidays, but after
Grandpa died, we mostly stopped that.

As for Bettina, she'd always viewed church as a place to
show off her clothes and jewelry. After all, a small town like ours
didn't offer nearly enough social occasions. She'd been known to
get up and make a dramatic exit if the sermon went on too long.
I'd always been so embarrassed to be dragged down the aisle
after her, with everyone watching, while the priest was still
talking. I was surprised she hadn't left instructions in her will to
be wheeled out of her own funeral early.

I was about to approach the altar when I heard a sound that
made my arm hairs prickle. *Tic-tic-tic-tic-scritch.* It was coming
from the side aisle where the confessional booths looked
simultaneously welcoming and sinister. Two small cubicles
hunched against the church wall, draped in heavy curtains. I took
a step closer. *Tic-tic-tic-tic-scritch.* I crept more quietly toward
the confessionals and was about yank the curtain back on the

priest's side when the noise changed. *Tic-tic-tic-tic – sigh – scritch.*

I twitched back the edge of the drape and peered in. Krampus sat in the priest's chair with his chin propped in one palm like a pouting kid. His other hand lay on the ledge for the priest's prayer book. He glanced at me as his claws performed their little dance. From forefinger to pinky: *tic-tic-tic-tic*. Then the thumb, rather than tapping the wood, dragged its claw along the wood: *scritch*. He looked away from me and sighed again.

"What if I had been the priest?" I said.

"Perhaps you cannot smell a priest from two miles away, but I can. Your church has not often been kind to pagans like myself."

"It's not my church. Anyway, how can you even come in here? Aren't you some kind of …" *Demon*, I was going to say, but that seemed rude. Especially as I didn't know what he was.

He snorted. "I am not a coward."

"I didn't mean–"

"No. I am only being sour."

I didn't know what to say and he didn't look at me. I let the curtain fall back in place.

Tic-tic-tic-tic-scritch.

I pulled back the other curtain and knelt inside. When I closed the curtain, the only light seemed to come from the priest's compartment. I folded my hands and said, "Bless me, Father, for I have sinned. It has been at least ten years since my last confession. I fornicated with a pagan …"

I meant it to be a joke, but when I looked through the grill to see his reaction, Krampus looked like some heartbreaking Renaissance painting. A soft halo of light fell around him and his ears, which were normally upright alongside his horns, drooped sadly. His eyelashes swept across his cheek as he looked down. He was not amused.

"Are you alright?"

He sighed but didn't tap his claws.

"What's wrong?"

I felt then how small the confessional was, how hard the kneeler was. Cold crept through my tights and into my legs. I could hear Krampus breathing unevenly. Because he was angry? Or sad?

"Peter?" Nothing. "Krampus?"

I was about to get up and go to him when he said, "It is only that I have lost so much … and I do not know how to gain it back."

"We'll find your trinket. I promise."

"But not only that. So many children who should have been punished and were not and grew to be very bad men. I have been reading all these things that happened while I was charmed. Terrible wars. This Hitler. Who ought to have been a good Bavarian boy, but then did such terrible things."

"Wait," I said. I really wanted to reverse everything he'd said, but at the very least, I needed him to stop so that I could catch up. "So, Hitler? You just heard about him?"

"No, no, but what he became. He was no worse a boy than many boys, but still, should I not have been to whip him? If I had known what was in his heart?"

"And you didn't punish him?"

"How could I? I was charmed. But then that was my own fault for being careless. Oh that horrible little girl." He moaned and put his head down on his arm. I put my hand to the grill, knowing he couldn't see me through it.

"My grandmother? Her charm kept you from punishing Hitler?"

"No. And yes. But no. So many things I should have done and could not."

"Wow." I wanted to say something more than that, but it blew my mind.

I'd known Bettina was evil, but you don't like to think your grandmother somehow helped Hitler. Plus, my brain was still trying to process what he meant about being "charmed."

"And they have forgotten me. Children are so wicked now. Do you know that when I come to punish them, they are not afraid? Not until I strike with the birches. I have been gone so long, of course they have forgotten me."

"So where did you go when you were charmed?" I said.

"No place at all."

"For how long?"

"So many years I do not know."

At least eighty years. Maybe more, depending on how old Bettina was when she cut off his beard. I was never going to complain about her ruining my Christmases again. No wonder he'd been so pissed off when he showed up in my bedroom.

"I'm sorry," I said.

"You have done nothing to apologize for, Moritza. You have been very kind to me." His voice dropped. Less mournful. More suggestive. "So very kind."

"Kiss me." I felt silly, but I pressed my lips to the grille and for an instant felt the warmth of his breath.

He shifted in his cubicle and then swept the curtain back. I thought he was leaving, but two clattering hops of his hooves later, he pulled back the drape to my cubicle. He was so dark, he was nothing but a shadow as he stepped into the confessional with me and pulled the curtain closed.

There was no room for two people. After all, privacy was the whole point of the confessional. I stood up, laughing, about to push him back outside, when he kissed me. It was a slow, sneaking, teasing kiss, his tongue flicking at the corners of my mouth, as the trailing ends of his beard slipped down into my cleavage. It made my stomach feel fluttery and my head light. At the same time, his hands began to sneak around me, testing the boundaries of my dress. He found the zipper, toyed with it, then dismissed it.

Then he kissed my neck and nipped at my ears, tormenting me with his tongue. It never went into my ears, a thing that would have set me squealing, but it danced around the edges and lapped at my earlobes.

Having given up on the dress' zipper, he slid his hands down my legs until he found the hem. As his hands came slithering back up my legs, his claws dragged along my stockings, popping open ladders in the thin fabric, sending little prickles along my skin. His hands reached my hips, then slid around to my butt, snagging and tearing as they went. I thought I should stop him. It had to be getting near eleven o'clock and we were in a confessional. When he dug his nails into my buttocks, though, I gasped and put my arms around his neck.

Until then, it had all been on him, but I couldn't blame him once I had my arms around him, and my mouth back on his. He pressed me into the wall of the confessional, grinding against me, so that I could feel the heat of him and the power of his thighs pressed against mine. And his cock. God, his cock, right there, thrusting against my belly.

More of my hose and my panties shredded under his nails and then I felt the electrical contact between my pubic hair and his fur. Little static shocks that slid into the quick of me and left my legs quivering. Desperate for him to touch me, I tried to spread my legs further, but there was no room to maneuver. I would have put my foot up on the kneeler, but he'd made such a mess of my hose that I couldn't figure out how to get out of them.

One evil sneaking claw snicked between my legs. It should have been terrifying, the way he teased at my clit with his claw, but it felt so amazing I didn't protest. Amazing, but dangerous, especially when he snagged at the hood and tugged at it. Not until it hurt, but until it made me gasp. Just enough to make my cunt go dripping wet, running down the inside of my leg.

Knowing he was strong enough to take my weight, I held tight to his neck and lifted myself a few inches. He growled against my mouth and lifted me higher so that his cock slid into the gap between my legs. He trembled from head to hoof, and for a second I thought he was going to lose his grip on me. After that shudder, though, he dug his nails deeper into my ass and lifted me more, pressing harder against me. It was so close to what I wanted, feeling the slippery heat of his cock brush against my clitoris, but it was still so far away, tangled up as I was.

Just my luck. I pushed him back and he let me slide far enough down the wall that my feet touched the floor again. When I tried to pull him back to me, he resisted. His face was so dark I couldn't tell what his expression was, but when I reached for his cock, he groaned and leaned his head back so that his horns scraped against the low ceiling of the confessional. I wanted him so badly I wasn't gentle. I squeezed his shaft and stroked it hard once, twice, three times, and then he grunted and pushed my hand away.

I was so confused I didn't know what to do. So I did what I wanted to do.

I turned around, hiked my dress up to my waist, and bent forward over the prie-dieu. His answer was immediate and destructive. He tore away the remains of my panties and tights until I was bare and accessible. That was all I cared about. He went down on his knees in that narrow space and sank his teeth

87

into the right side of my ass. Hard enough I knew I was going to have bruises and maybe teeth marks. When his tongue whipsawed between my legs, I almost screamed with frustration. I was so wet and agitated and I wanted. I wanted.

"Oh god, please. Just fuck me. Please."

He stood up and grabbed me by the hips.

"Such a dirty mouth," he hissed. "So dirty."

"Fuck me."

I could tell he meant to do it slowly, to ease into me. For a few seconds the tip of his shaft teased against my pussy. His tail lashed furiously, thumping against the paneled walls and beating at the curtain.

"Ah, so wet," he said. Then he clearly gave up on slow and put it home in one thrust. Whatever I'd thought it might be like, it was a thousand times better. Those ridges running down the underside of his cock hammered against my clit so fast it sent a tremor all the way into my pussy. When he pulled out, the tremor came tumbling back, and then redoubled with the next thrust. For a second I thought about that old bridge shaken apart by wind resonance. If he hit my natural resonance, would I fall apart?

The answer, about four thrusts later was yes. What had been a tremor became this thundering pleasure that boomed in my ears and made me bite my lip to keep quiet. He wasn't done and it all began to build again, his fur rubbing against my rump, his cock stroking in and out of me, throbbing so hard I could feel it in the blood hammering past my eardrums. I hiked my right leg up, high enough to rest my knee on the prie-dieu, so that I was teetering on one unfamiliar high-heeled shoe. He pounded deeper into me, filled me so tight I could barely breathe. Or that was from having my cheek pressed to the wall of the confessional, or having his arms wrapped so tightly around me that my ribs hurt. Whatever made it difficult to breathe, his cock thrashed and thumped in me, as wild as his tongue and just as powerful. I pressed down and tilted my hips to take every thrust hard against my clit. I felt the coming tide of another orgasm and gave myself up to it.

When it hit, I was not quiet. He clamped his hand over my mouth and I let him, gasping in the slightly salty taste of his palm as I came, hot, wet and helpless. Whatever control he had over me, he had none over himself. He thrust hard enough to knock my head into the wall, and I felt his legs go rubbery, so that we tilted off balance. One of his legs kicked uncontrollably and his hoof thudded against the prie-dieu. I had to catch the edge of the door frame to keep us from falling right through the curtain and out into the chapel.

I couldn't help myself. The sound of him gasping and his hooves clattering on the floor for purchase set me to giggling.

"Ch-ch, you wicked girl," he scolded, but I could hear him smiling.

"I can't believe you just seduced me in a church."

"*Nein*! This was your doing. It was you who said such lewd things."

"But you–"

A rattle and a clunk came from outside our cave, followed by the sound of footsteps in the foyer. Father Dalton.

"Oh crap," I whispered. "The priest is here."

I spent a few precious seconds wrestling with the remains of my panties and hose. I stepped out of my shoes, stripped the shredded nylon off, and stepped back into the shoes. Thankfully I reached for a handful of tissues out of the box I'd knocked off the prie-dieu. No doubt put there for godly souls come to confession, but I used them to clean up the aftermath of my godless fucking.

I handed the remains of my undergarments and the soiled wad of tissues to Krampus, ignoring his puzzled looked. Then I smoothed my dress down and stepped out, just as Father Dalton came up the aisle. He wasn't alone.

"Ah, Moritza!" Father Dalton looked startled, but the man behind him didn't seem surprised. The man didn't exactly look like a stranger either. I knew him from somewhere. Did he work for the funeral parlor?

"Um, what time is it?" I said.

"Just now ten-thirty. The florist is here. Did you want to confess?"

"What? Oh, no, I was just trying to enjoy a little quiet time."

"I understand. I'm sure this week has been very trying for you."

I answered with a smile, because I wasn't sure *trying* quite covered the last week. I was ready for it to be over.

"Oh, I'm sorry. Since you were asking, this is Moritza Holenkranz, the deceased's granddaughter," Father Dalton said to the man behind him. "I didn't catch your name."

"Jones," the man said. "I was a friend of your grandmother's."

"Oh." I didn't bother to hide my disbelief. Like hell, he'd been Bettina's friend. She didn't have any friends.

He put his hand out to me, and to stall for time, I shook it. He really was familiar. He was a few inches shorter than me, and he wore dark glasses and a tailored suit that helped camouflage the size of his belly.

"I was hoping we would have a few minutes to talk before the service," Jones said.

Before I could say no or make an excuse, Father Dalton said, "You're welcome to use my office. It's just down the hall there, past the restrooms."

"You're so kind." Jones performed a tricky maneuver, skirting around me so that he could herd me toward Father Dalton's office. As he circled me, he sniffed at the air. Actually lifted his nose and inhaled. Was it glaringly obvious that I'd just had sex in the confessional? I guessed not, because Father Dalton didn't seem to notice. He gave us a wave and hurried down the side aisle.

I was expecting Jones to start in with casual chit-chat, but he didn't say anything while we walked toward the priest's office.

Only once we were inside and the door was closed did he say, "A most unusual perfume. But pleasant. A touch of clove, isn't there?"

I turned around and found him smiling harmlessly at me. Still, the way he'd gone right for that made me nervous. Like he knew something.

"I hope you won't consider it presumptuous of me to name Mrs. von Holenkranz as a friend. In truth, our relationship was a bit more professional. I'm a dealer of art and antiquities, with a particular emphasis on jewelry of unusual provenance. She hired me for a few acquisitions, and we had discussed some items she was considering selling. I wondered if she had mentioned–"

"Look, I don't know anything about any of that right now."

"Ah, well, of course, I imagine it will take some time for you to familiarize yourself with the contents of Mrs. von Holenkranz' estate. I simply wanted to introduce myself so that at some future point, we might discuss any items you might wish to part with."

With a practiced flourish, he produced a business card and offered it to me between his first two fingers. I took it and was surprised to see that it said, "Reginald H. Jones, Appraiser." I'd just assumed Jones was a fake name.

"Thanks, Mr. Jones. Have we met before?"

"I don't believe so. I'm sure I would have remembered meeting such a charming young lady."

Maybe Jones wasn't a fake name, but that line of bullshit was fake as hell. I'd never been called charming, because I wasn't. Especially at that moment I was all too aware that I looked like a raggedy hoyden. That was Bettina's word.

"Well, Mr. Jones, I really need to get ready for the funeral." What I meant was, "Maybe we could put off the business talk until after I get the old lady buried."

I think he took my meaning, because he gave me a nod and a smile.

"Of course, Miss von Holenkranz. My condolences."

"Just Holenkranz. Not von Holenkranz," I said.

He nodded again and then carefully backed out of Father Dalton's office, like he was in the presence of royalty. Alone at last, I tried to get my shit together. I walked down to the ladies room and looked myself over. On the upside, my hair was always a frizzy disaster area, so that didn't matter. On the downside, the dress that had been freshly ironed two hours ago was rumpled and covered in stray hairs. At least the hairs were black, or I would have needed a whole roll of tape to solve the problem. All I could really do was retie the scarf Gram had given me to hold the hair chaos at bay. Then I washed my hands, and used some damp paper towels to wipe my dress and legs down.

I hoped I looked presentable enough, but when I walked back to the foyer, Gram was coming in. As she shrugged out of her coat, she frowned at me. Even while I was hugging her, she frowned at me.

"Didn't I just iron that dress?" she said.

"Yes. I guess it didn't take."

"What happened to your tights?"

I stared at her for second, because I couldn't think of a lie fast enough. "They were, uh, they were making my legs itch so I took them off." Right along with my panties. Frankly, my naughty bits were still tingling.

"Are you okay?" Gram gave me a concerned look.

"Yeah, I just want to get this over with."

I wanted that even more once I walked into the chapel and saw what I'd done. It was a good thing Bettina was dead, because I had committed a travesty against anything like good taste. The black casket with the red lining, the red roses, the red dress, the mink, the jewelry, it was ghastly and tacky and hideous. Like some homemade production of a horror movie. I half-expected Bettina to sit up like the Crypt Keeper and narrate.

"Oh my," Gram said.

"I didn't realize it would look so …"

"*Phantom of the Opera*?"

"Elvira, Mistress of the Dark."

Gram choke-snorted into her hand and tried to camouflage it as a cough. She laid her hand on my shoulder and said, "It's okay, sweetie. Almost nobody will see it."

She was right. As we got closer to eleven o'clock, a few people trickled in and took up seats in the empty chapel. Bettina's doctor, her lawyer, Vandy Harris, and then Mr. Jones, who apparently planned to wear his sunglasses during the funeral. Danny the Dickhead was there, too. It turned out he worked half-time for the county coroner and half-time for the funeral parlor.

Seeing him again jarred me back on track. Once the funeral was taken care of, I had to focus on finding Krampus' bead. And Danny was on the list of people who'd been in Bettina's house

94

the night the bead went missing. That meant I was going to have to talk to him, because I wasn't breaking into anyone else's house. I couldn't deal with that shit again.

The last person to arrive for the funeral was a tall man in a black suit and fedora. The way he was dressed, I assumed he worked for the funeral parlor, too, so I was already turning toward the chapel, when Gram said, "Oh, Peter! You're such a sweetheart to come."

My head snapped back on a swivel.

While the man in black was in my peripheral vision, he was Krampus, but as soon as I turned to face him head on, he was just a man in a black suit. I don't know that I would have recognized him on the street. Yes, he was taller than most men, and his feet were maybe on the small side for a man his size. He had a thick mustache and a glossy, untrimmed black beard than hung down to the knot in his tie. As he removed his hat, shaggy hair brushed over his shoulders.

Even as he reached for Gram's hand with one hairy-knuckled hand, I still don't think I would have known him, except for his eyes. In that stranger's face, were Krampus' flashing black eyes framed by ridiculous eyelashes. He met my gaze, to gauge my reaction. I think my mouth was hanging open, but Gram was too distracted to notice.

"Oh, you silly boy. Give me a hug." Gram bypassed his outstretched hand and wrapped her arms around him.

After he hugged her, he came to me and kissed my mouth, then my temple, then the top of my head. I buried my face in his chest and found my cheek pressed against an unusually soft suit. Heat radiated off him as though he were naked and above all, no matter what he looked like, he smelled like Krampus.

"I think Father Dalton's ready. We better go in," Gram said.

I let Krampus take my hand and lead me toward the chapel. As we walked, he leaned down and whispered, "In English, you have this word. *Glamer*. A charm to fool the eye. That is all it is." I understood then how he had come and played cards with Gram. Sat around drinking and telling dirty jokes, dressed up in a human suit. A human *glamour*. I nodded, feeling like I'd been sucker punched.

I sat down with him on one side and Gram on the other, and once we were seated, Father Dalton started the service. Whenever we stood and sang or knelt and prayed, Krampus followed our movements, but he obviously didn't know what any of it meant. A pagan. Once, when he bowed his head, I saw the faint shimmer of ghostly horns rising up from his head. When I blinked, they were gone. For most of the service, he rested his arm across the back of the pew and toyed with the curls of hair on the back of my neck.

At one point, Jones turned in his seat and looked at me. Then he did a double-take, and I knew he was looking at Krampus, whose hand went still on the back of my neck. For a good ten seconds, the two of them stared at each other, before Jones turned around in his seat and faced forward again.

"Who is that?" Gram whispered.

"Mr. Jones. He – Bettina – he's an antiques dealer." As soon as I said it, I thought of how he had described himself. "With a particular emphasis on jewelry of unusual provenance."

Jewelry of an unusual provenance. Would an enchanted bead carved of reindeer horn qualify? Suddenly his appearance at Bettina's funeral seemed even creepier.

Chapter Seven

Here Comes Santa Claus

At a normal funeral, there would be crying and after it was over, everybody would come by and hug the grieving family. At Bettina's funeral, there was just quiet, except for Gram's whispering. When it was over, people walked by and mumbled vague things.

"I hope everything's all okay," Vandy said when it was her turn.

Mr. Jones flashed me an awkward smile as he passed me in the foyer. Half condolence, half vulture-like hope. Did he know about Krampus' bead? As for Krampus, he'd pulled his disappearing act as soon as the service was over. To avoid Jones?

"He's an odd bird," Gram said, after Jones had walked away. "He seems awfully familiar."

"Really? Have you seen him before?"

"It sure seems like it, but I can't think of where."

So it wasn't just me.

Danny went by on an errand to get Bettina ready to go out to the cemetery. I hurried after him and said, "Hey, can I talk to you?"

"Uh, sure," he said, but he gave me a weasely look. Or he just naturally looked like a weasel. He kept walking until we reached the side door out to the alley, where he stopped, waiting for me to talk.

"Look, something went missing out of my grandmother's bedroom the night she died. It's kind of important. I mean, it's not worth any money, but it's important. So if maybe you ended up with–"

"What's that supposed to mean? You think I fucking stole something?" The fact that his hackles went up immediately made me think that he was a thief or that his childhood reputation as a dickhead had followed him into adulthood and left him defensive.

"I didn't say that. It's the sort of thing a person could pick up, not thinking it was anything important."

"Well, I don't just *pick stuff up*." He tried to step past me, but I cut him off before he could get to the door. He smelled like sweat and too much aftershave.

"I'm not accusing you of anything. I just need to find this thing. It's a bead. Carved out of horn. It's like as big as a marble, maybe. Something that'd be easy to lose and easy to pick up."

"Well, if it's so important, you shoulda been more careful with it, I guess."

He hit me hard with his shoulder and yanked the door open. I watched him stomp out to the hearse and begin rooting around in it. I turned and walked back toward the chapel. Behind me, I heard the door open again. I looked back, thinking it would be Danny coming in, but it was Mr. Jones. Going out. Mr. Jones going out. Because he'd been standing in the shadows at the end of the hallway the whole time I was talking to Danny.

I tried to talk Gram out of going to the cemetery with me, but she said I shouldn't have to go alone. It was such a miserably cold day, I wished we'd both stayed away by the time it was over. We stood out in the cold, the wind slapping against my bare legs, and watched Bettina's very expensive coffin get winched into a grave, while the funeral director and Danny the Dickhead stood by trying to look professionally mournful. Danny couldn't pull it off, because he kept glaring at me and then frowning and scratching at his neck. The way people do when their neck doesn't itch but they're thinking really hard about something.

Jones followed us out to the cemetery, too, but he stayed at his car, talking to his driver. He'd worn his sunglasses in the church for the funeral, but outside with the sun glinting off the snow, he pushed the glasses up on his head. While he and his driver talked, they watched us. Jones stood with his hands in his pockets, stretching his suit jacket tight over his belly. Once the coffin was in the ground and the cemetery workers got ready to fill the grave, Jones got into his car.

"Hang on, Gram, I'll be back in a sec," I said.

Cursing those stupid high heels, I started out across the cemetery, headed for Jones' car. His driver had turned it around and was creeping back toward the main gate. I picked up my pace and reached the curb just as the beige sedan rolled past. Jones' sunglasses were still pushed up on his head, and as the car accelerated past me, I saw his eyes. He was smiling, about to wave, but when I saw his eyes, he saw my face. Frowning, he jerked his hand back and shoved his dark glasses back down over his eyes, but it was too late. I knew those washed out eyes gone yellow from illness or hard living. He was the Santa from Bettina's party.

"Hey!" I yelled, but Jones' driver kept going, picking up speed as he pulled out onto the main road.

I hiked back to Gram with my heart pounding and a nasty taste in my mouth. Not just the Santa from Bettina's party, but the Santa I'd seen as I walked away from Vandy Harris' house. Who the hell was he? What did he want? I was pretty sure I already knew that answer, whether I wanted to or not.

"What was that about?" Gram said when I got back to her and the waiting limo.

"Oh, nothing. Just that weird Jones guy. He wants to buy some of Bettina's jewelry."

"Not that we're exactly in mourning, but it's still awfully rude for him to talk business at the funeral. And to follow you out here to the cemetery."

"Yeah, he's kind of a creep," I said, grateful that she was going to let it go.

It was nearly four in the afternoon by the time we got home. I wrestled out of the new dress that I never planned to wear again and took a long hot shower to get some of the feeling back in my legs. Then Gram and I sat watching the dregs of Christmas TV until it got dark. I kept thinking that if I laid the facts out in my head, I could make sense of it all. Basically, I was kidding myself, because what I had for facts were some old photos, a missing diary, and a sore butt from where Krampus had bitten me.

At about seven, Gram went into the kitchen and started scrounging in the fridge, looking at leftovers.

"There's still some ham," she called. "But the potatoes are done for."

"Why don't I go into town and get some Chinese? I can get you some more scotch, too, since Peter drank yours." That's how bad I had it, looking for an excuse to say his name.

"Oh, that sounds magnificent." She came to the kitchen door, smiling. "I do like that boy. It was so funny, the first time I saw him out of costume with that big beard and all that hair. I'd assumed it was part of the costume. Something he could take off. But I have to say he knows how to dress. I'm not sure about those pointy Italian mobster shoes, but the hat is very classy."

I didn't really feel like getting dressed again and driving back into town, but I wanted to do something nice for Gram, since she'd spent her whole day helping me get Bettina buried. It was when I was standing in the liquor store that a new idea presented itself to me. I could go by Danny's house, see what he was up to. I'd take him a bottle of something, just to make it look like a friendly visit. He didn't strike me as a scotch man, so I got him a bottle of Jack Daniels Black. Nice, but not fancy.

As I drove out to his house, I thought about calling to tell Gram I'd be a little later with dinner, but I didn't want to have to explain to her what I was doing. I figured I'd just do it short and sweet. Present the bottle as an apology, explain how I'd left the bead sitting on the nightstand and maybe it had been misplaced while they were moving Bettina's body. Just ask him to think if there was some way it had ended up at the morgue or something. Offer to pay him to look for it. I figured if I presented him with a plausible story and a reward, it would all work out.

There were three cars parked in front of his house when I pulled up. I hoped the bottle would get me an invitation inside, so I held it front and center when I knocked on the door. I could hear a low conversation like the TV on the news, and then the curtain beside the door twitched. Then the curtain on the window to the dining room moved, too. So I was getting vetted before they opened the door?

I was starting to get annoyed so I knocked again. The door opened, but whoever answered it was standing behind it.

"Danny?" I said. I stepped into the room and took it in all at once. Danny and his folks sitting on the couch, staring at me. Their hands were tied together in front of them. Then I knew who would be behind the door. Jones. Whoever or whatever Jones was.

I dropped the bottle of Jack and ran. Jones came after me so fast, I couldn't even look back. I didn't dare head back to the car. It was so old the doors had manual locks and they were all unlocked. I wouldn't have time to lock the doors and get the car started before he got to me. So I ran down the road and cut into a pasture. I heard his feet pounding behind me and ran faster. I wasn't any kind of runner. Never ran for sport or exercise. I was just counting on youth and fear to give me the edge. Except it wasn't. He was gaining on me. *Inconceivable*! How was a fifty-year-old fat guy in a suit gaining on me?

With a sickening thump in the bottom of my stomach, I remembered about Krampus' glamour. What if that old paunchy man look was a glamour? What if the thing coming after me was something as strange and powerful as Krampus? What if Jones wasn't playing at Santa? What if he *was* Santa? That was insane, except that I was running as fast as I could, hoping I wasn't about to have a meet and greet with a barbed wire fence in the dark, and he was practically right behind me.

As Peter had said, Santa was no friend of his. Maybe Santa wanted him locked up again. So he was coming after the trinket. And me.

I kept running, but my side was starting to hurt and my lungs burned every time I inhaled. I was staggering on clods of dirt, while Jones crunched over the dead corn stalks, getting closer with every second. I managed half a dozen more strides before something solid struck me in the back and sent me sprawling into the dirt, knocking the wind out of me. I tried to get my hands under me to get up, but Jones kept me pinned down.

"Heh. That was a pretty good run," he said.

Not Jones. Not Santa. From the sound of it, a younger guy. A runner. An elf? After a minute, he stood up, but he kept a good grip on my coat collar. "Now, you can behave and walk back or I'll knock you out and drag you back."

"I'll walk," I said. I thought I might get a chance to escape, but the truth was I didn't have the energy for it. Whoever the guy was, he was in a lot better shape than I was. I trudged along beside him, keeping up because I had to. If I slowed down at all, he nearly choked me with my coat. When we got back to Danny's house, the front porch smelled like whiskey. The shattered bottle of Jack lay where I'd dropped it.

Jones grinned when I walked through the door. His eyes were the same putrid yellow I remembered, and looking into them made gooseflesh crawl up my arms to my neck. Just like me, he was twenty years older, but he still looked exactly the same. Really, the only difference between that scary childhood Santa and this guy was that the alleged antiquities dealer had a gun in his hand.

Another guy stepped out of the dining room and closed the front door. Jones' driver. He was older than the guy who'd chased me down, but he looked tougher. Squinty. I think the correct term is *goon*. He looked like a goon. He had a gun, too.

"Ah, Miss Holenkranz. So glad you could join us. Please, sit down." Jones gestured me toward the couch with the gun.

With the elf-thug breathing down my neck, I walked over and squeezed in next to Danny's mother. She used to make these awesome carrot cupcakes that she brought to school for Danny's birthday when we were in grade school.

"What do you want?" I said.

Jones sneered at me. "You know exactly what I want. And unless you have something helpful to contribute, please keep quiet while we work."

The runner fished a zip tie out of his pocket and tied my hands in my lap. I took a good look at him, trying to decide if he was an elf. He was short and his ears were pointy-ish, but that was about it. Maybe he was just a run-of-the-mill thug, unless he was wearing a glamour, too. I was pretty sure that I had lost my mind.

After my wrists were tied, the elf-thug went back to stand at the front door, while Jones and the goon walked out of the room. A few minutes later, I heard the nature of their work: searching the house. They went from room to room and tore them apart.

The Diekaters and I sat on the couch, staring at our hands or sometimes at the athletic elf, who seemed perfectly content to stand at the door and glare back at us. From looking at Danny and his father, I could tell that they'd put up a fight. Danny had a black eye and his dad had a bloody nose and a cut on his cheekbone.

I knew Gram would start wondering where I was, and at the one-hour mark, my cell phone rang in my coat pocket.

"Don't touch it," the elf said. "You just sit still."

He shifted his down jacket away from his hip far enough to show me that he had a gun, too. So I sat still and let the phone ring through to voicemail. Mrs. Diekater started crying quietly. After a few minutes, the phone beeped to let me know I had a new message.

It rang again at the two-hour mark, and that was when Jones came back to the living room. Down the hallway, I could hear the other guy still tearing stuff apart.

Jones was as sweaty and flushed as I felt still bundled up in my coat.

"Her phone's been ringing," the elf said with a chin nod at me.

"Well, let's see who's been calling."

Jones fished around in my pockets, all business. He managed to get the cell phone out of my inside pocket without even touching my boob. He stepped back out of my reach and pushed some buttons on my phone.

"Ah, 'Gram.' That's your maternal grandmother, yes?"

"Yeah. Who are you?" I said.

"Oh, you don't remember me? Well, that's not too surprising as we've only met once before. The Christmas after your parents died. You were rather small."

"Oh, I remember that. I remember you played Santa at that party."

"I'm hurt. I'm no two-bit Santa impersonator." My stomach twisted around as I waited for him to drop the terrible news that he was Santa. Instead, he said, "I'm your uncle, Moritza."

I was about to say, "The hell you are," when I realized what he meant. Not my uncle. My step-uncle. I did the math and took a guess.

"Your father was…Bettina's Husband Number Five?" I said.

"Four. So you do remember me?"

"What do you want with the bead?"

"What do you think I want?"

"Really, I don't have a clue," I said. "I know my grandmother used it to avoid punishment when she was a little girl. Is that it? You want to steal the charm because you don't want to be punished for something you did when you were a kid?"

"For the record, I have no interest in stealing anything. That charm was promised to me."

"Funny, that wasn't in Bettina's will."

"She promised it to me when I was a young man. As payment. I *earned* it," he said.

I looked at him harder then, because I was still trying to link him up to the right husband. The right set of stories. Then it hit me, what he'd done to earn something like that from Bettina.

"Hunting accident, right?" I said.

"Pardon?"

"You father died in a hunting accident, right? That's how you earned the charm? Number Four had all those oil wells and liked to hunt." It occurred to me that Bettina would have inherited Number Four's oil wells. And now I had inherited them. I tried a different angle: "Is that what you want? The oil wells? Or the money? You can have it."

Jones smiled in this completely terrifying way. Greed and emptiness and something that was maybe just the banality of evil.

"Money is nothing. I can get money. What I want is the charm," he said. He pulled the gun out of his pocket and, still smiling, pointed it at Danny's head.

109

"He doesn't know anything," I said. "For that matter, I don't know anything."

"Don't test my patience, young lady. I overheard you discussing the bead with Mr. Diekater at your grandmother's funeral today."

"Yeah, but like I told her, I didn't take it. I never even saw it," Danny said. His mother started shaking, which made me feel shaky, with her shoulder trembling against mine.

"And I told you not to bother opening your mouth if you weren't going to be helpful," Jones snapped.

"He doesn't know," I said.

"And that's why you were so eager to discuss it with him that you came here tonight bearing gifts of alcohol?" The gun shifted and pointed at me.

"I came here to apologize. I didn't want Danny to think I was accusing him of stealing anything."

"Yet you did just that. Or did I misunderstand your conversation? The bead, you said, was on the night table. And then it disappeared. Logic dictates, it was removed by someone. If you don't know where it is, then someone else who was at the house that night must."

"Okay then, smartypants. Why don't you tell me where it is?" I said.

Jones chuckled and lowered the gun.

"Let us see. Ms. Harris was entirely ignorant, and it was clear to me that she was telling the truth."

"You went and saw Vandy?"

"My dear, you led me right to her," Jones said. So he had been the Santa I passed on her street.

I'd been worried someone would catch me breaking in. I never thought about someone watching me on purpose.

"Mr. Bertram also knew nothing."

"Mr. Bert – Digger? You went and messed with Digger? If you hurt him, I'm going to put your ass in a vise."

"I have hurt no one, Miss Holenkranz. Yet. It's obvious to me that you do not know where the item I'm seeking is. Though I must assume it was you who so foolishly opened the vial which contained the charm?"

Jones reached into his suit pocket and took out the stupid thing. I couldn't even remember where I'd left it, which I guess made me the idiot. Had I left it in my bedroom at Bettina's? Or at Gram's? That made my stomach roll over. But no, he hadn't had time to go to Gram's. I hadn't been gone that long.

"Yes, Miss Holenkranz?"

"Yes what?"

"You opened it? And unstrung the bead?"

"Yes," I said. The gun was still down as Jones held up the gold cylinder.

"Stupid girl. Do you know that monster is out there free because of you?"

"That monster is a friend of mine." Was he? I didn't really know, and that must have been obvious, because Jones snorted.

"Your delusions regarding the Krampus aside, let's return to the more important matter of where is the rest of the charm? You

111

clearly believe Mr. Diekater stole the bead, and I have ruled out the other possibilities, so I must assume he still has it. Somewhere."

"I didn't steal it!" Danny looked defiant, but when Jones brought the gun up and pointed it at Danny's mom, he looked scared.

"Let's try again. I'm quite adept at sorting lies from truth, and it was clear to me when you spoke to Miss Holenkranz at the funeral that you were lying."

"Not a bead. I didn't steal any bead. I swear. I took some earrings, okay? Some plain diamond earrings. Digger stepped out on the balcony to smoke while I finished bagging the body. I took the earrings. To give to my girlfriend for Christmas."

"Jesus Christ, Danny! You stole my grandmother's earrings before her corpse was even cold?" I said.

"I'm sorry, but fuck. You got money. And it wasn't like she needed them anymore."

"Wow."

"I'm sorry, but that's all I took. I didn't take this bead charm thing," Danny said.

My phone rang again.

"Looks like dear old Gram is worrying about you," Jones said. "Are you going to keep her waiting or are you going to help me find the charm? Do we need to pay her a visit?"

"If I knew where the trinket was, I would have already given it back to Krampus. I wouldn't give it to you," I said.

"Because he's your friend?"

"Yes." At that moment, I knew it was true, because I heard the answer coming: *clip-clop-crunch*. Krampus walking across the porch and stepping on broken glass.

The elf turned around and put his hand on the gun holstered under his coat. Just as he was about to reach for the doorknob, the front door snapped open and plowed him right in the face. He fell backward and landed like sack of bricks. He didn't get up.

Jones and the goon both spun around and pointed their guns at the doorway. My heart went up in my throat, because I didn't know whether Krampus understood about guns. The last time he was out and about in the world, did people have the kind of guns we had now? Were there goons back then?

He didn't seem worried when he stepped through the doorway. If anything, he looked amused. Over his shoulder, he had his satchel full of chains, and in his right hand he held his birches. He lifted one hoof and shook it. To shed some snow? Or some whiskey and broken glass? Then he closed the door and daintily stepped around the fallen thug.

"Stop right there," the goon said.

"What the fuck is that?" Danny's dad said.

"I am Krampus." He bowed to the Diekaters and tamped the end of his birches on the floor.

"I see you haven't found the bead yet either," Jones said.

"No. But I am no longer charmed, Simon David Butterman."

For a few seconds Jones looked shocked. Then he laughed.

"That's very impressive."

Krampus set down his satchel and let the chains spill out as he retrieved his little book. Propping the birches against the side of his leg, he flipped the book open and considered it.

"There are very many entries in my book beside your name, Simon Butterman. Theft. Insolence. A dog poisoned. A girl interfered with in a most disgraceful way. And then at last, yes, murder. An act to turn the others into trifles. And you, Mario Alfredi."

The older goon's eyes almost popped out of his head, but Krampus didn't look at him. He just flipped the pages of his book some more.

"Ch-ch. So many petty cruelties that there is not time enough for me to list them just now. In all earnestness, I am surprised that you boys would come looking for me. I expected that I would have to search for you, yet here you are."

"Here I am," Jones said, "but I'm not exactly here for you."

"No, that's so. You're here for my trinket. But you were not so clever as the girl who stole it first."

"It looks to me like I've been pretty clever–"

"To have tied up my Moritza and come face to face with me, armed with only that toy?"

"*That toy* is a GLOCK and I guarantee it'll put a hole through you," the goon said.

Krampus turned a withering look on the guy and laughed. Not the fun, slightly goatish laugh, but laughter so derisive I got worried Mario might decide to put a bullet into Krampus.

"A hole in me. Very amusing." Krampus raised his hand to pretend to wipe a tear away. He started laughing again, and this time he leaned forward to press his hand to his thigh.

"You want me to shut this joker up?" Mario said.

Before Jones could answer, Krampus straightened up. This time instead of his book of sins, he held the end of a chain in his left hand. He swung it like a whip and struck Mario in the arm. The gun went flying and skittered across the floor. Maybe thinking he had time to dodge the chain, Jones stepped closer to Krampus just in time to take the birches full in the face. He still had his gun, but he was too busy screaming and pawing at his face to use it. Then the chain came down on him, once across the back and once on his skull.

Mario scrabbled across the floor after his gun, and Danny and I had the same thought, because we both stood up and went after it. Instead of helping, though, we caused more trouble. Mario got to the gun first, and then Danny and I were in the way.

"Moritza!" Krampus hissed. I ducked but Danny didn't. To get him out of the way, Krampus planted a hoof in his chest and shoved him back. He rebounded off the TV cabinet and landed hard on the floor.

I never knew a gun would be that loud, but when it went off, I thought I'd gone deaf. In this eerie twilight of silence, the chain rippled and clinked, more fluid than any chain should have been. It leapt out of Krampus' hand and smacked Mario in the face. Like a living thing, its tail coiled around the goon's throat. One sharp jerk on the chain brought him to the floor. He still had the

115

gun in his hand when he fell, but he gave it up after Krampus jumped on his back and started to work him over with the birches.

In the middle of the whipping, my hearing started to come back. Danny's mother was crying, Danny was groaning, Jones was whimpering, and Krampus was panting from the hard work. Slowly, he straightened up and looked around. Seeing that Jones and Mario were down for the count, he came to me. With a swipe of his claw, he cut the zip tie around my wrists.

"What is that thing?" Danny's dad said. I didn't blame him. It was hard to get your head around the idea of Krampus.

"Is everyone okay?" I said. That was all I could think of, that one bullet. Danny's folks seemed okay. Krampus was fine. I was okay. Mario and Jones were fucked up, but not shot. "Danny, are you okay?"

"Yeah, just winded," he said.

I started to crawl over to him when I saw it.

The cause of all this trouble.

The damned trinket.

With Danny sprawled out on the floor, I could see the heavy lug soles of his work boots. Trapped in one of the grooves like a pebble was what looked like an ivory marble.

"Look," I said.

Krampus squatted down beside me and looked. When he saw it, this wave of relief came over his face. His hand was shaking when he reached out and touched the bead. Using the tip of his claw to pry the bead out of the treads in Danny's boots, Krampus caught the loose bead in his hand. He looked like he might cry.

"Are you okay? It's okay now?" I said.

"*Ja. Alles ist gut.*"

I laid my hand on his arm, which was hot and damp from the exertion of fighting. He looked at me and then looked away, almost embarrassed.

"I need something to tie it," he said.

"Do you have some string or some yarn or something?" I asked Mrs. Diekater. She nodded, looking like a woman who was never going to blink again.

By then Danny's father had gotten a knife from the kitchen and cut his zip ties. After he freed his wife, she got up off the couch and pulled a sewing basket out of the bottom cupboard of the china hutch. She handed it to me from as far away from Krampus as she could. I dug in and grabbed the first thing that came to my hand that looked sturdy enough for the job: a skein of silk embroidery thread. He stood perfectly still while I gathered his beard into a braid, but he insisted on threading the bead onto it himself and tying it up with the embroidery floss. When it was finished, the bead hung securely, with a bright patch of sky blue silk to hold it.

He kept stroking his hand over it, like he was scared it would disappear, but after a few minutes, he looked around and took stock of the situation. Nudging Mario with one hoof, he said, "This one I will leave for you to deal with."

"Maybe we should call the police. Tell them these guys broke in here," I suggested.

Now that the goon was disarmed, though, the Diekaters didn't seem scared of him. Instead they were huddled up in the corner of the dining room, staring at Krampus like he was Satan himself. I wanted to explain that he wasn't, except that would have required me to be able to explain what he was.

While I was wondering about that, Krampus used his chains to bind Jones. Or Simon Butterman, whatever his name was. I went over to pat Jones' pockets and found what I expected: the small leather book he'd stolen from Bettina's safe.

"My grandmother had this. I think it's how she figured out what to do, to cut your beard," I said.

I admit that I was curious about the book, but when Krampus took it out of my hands, I was relieved, too. If I hadn't even been able to keep it secure in an actual safe, I didn't have any business owning it. Besides, something that dangerous shouldn't be floating around in the human world. We are not a species you should trust with anything like that.

Krampus scowled over the book for a few minutes before he tucked it into his satchel, along with his naughty and nice list. After tying the birches to his satchel, he swung it over his shoulder.

He stood in front of me for a moment, not speaking. I wasn't sure what to say, either. He had what he needed. He was free.

On the floor, the athletic goon groaned and tried to turn over. Before he could, I reached down and took the gun out of his holster. When I turned back to Krampus, he had lifted Jones and put him over his shoulder.

"The other two can go, but this one, his punishment is not yet sufficient."

"What will you do with him?" I said.

"Punish him further."

Krampus turned away from me and walked off into thin air.

Good-bye.

Chapter Eight

Let It Snow! Let It Snow! Let It Snow!

After all the stuff that happened at Christmas, I spent a few weeks saying I was just going to hire an auction company and have them come in and sell everything.

Eventually I got over that and realized that whatever else had happened, this was my hometown, and it might be handy to have my own house. Er, mansion. So instead of lounging in the sand for Spring Break, I was bagging up designer clothes and tagging them for donation. Tomorrow I was going to hit the office and start going through paperwork with Bettina's lawyer.

By the time we broke for lunch on the first day, we'd already spent five hours sorting through the closet, and you could hardly tell we'd done anything. The project was going to eat up all of my Spring Break and then some.

At noon I had to drop Gram off at home, because her back was hurting her.

"Well, I'm sorry I'm not more help to you," she said.

"I don't want you to overwork yourself. Vandy and I will get it taken care of."

We rode in silence for a while and then she said the same thing she'd said to me when my plane got in the night before. The same thing she'd been asking me for the last three months: "So, how's Peter? You know, I don't even know his last name."

"Black," I said.

"Peter Black. Well, how is he?"

"I don't know.

"Oh, you don't see him anymore?" Without looking at her, I knew Gram was making a sad face.

That's how much I'd been dodging her questions. I hadn't even confessed that in three months I hadn't seen him at all. He'd walked out of the Diekaters' front room and out of my life. Poof. Vanished.

"Oh, just not in a while," I said. What was wrong with me that I couldn't admit that he was gone?

"That's too bad."

"Well, you know, he's busy. I'm busy. It's hard to find time."

"I wish you would make some time for each other. I think he's a good man."

"Yeah," I said, but I didn't know what I thought he was. I wondered what he'd told her that she had these ideas about him.

I was mostly relieved that Gram went home, because at least I could work without her quizzing me about my non-existent boyfriend. I needed to stop dodging her questions and tell the truth. I was so over the George Glass game.

At six o'clock, Vandy Harris said she really had to get home. Then I was alone and the closet wasn't even cleaned out after ten hours of work. I kept at the last few things, like finding the right bags and boxes for various hats and pairs of shoes. Bettina was such a fricking clothes horse.

When I went to pee and stretch my legs an hour later, I looked out the window and saw that it was snowing. Nothing heavy, but probably the last dusting of the winter. It made me happy, in no small part because I was driving Gram's zippy little all-wheel drive Subaru. Great on the snow and no more dead batteries. It was nice being able to do some stuff for Gram.

Coming back down the hallway, I heard a strange *pop!* from downstairs. Then a crackling and a rustling. I crept toward the stairs, feeling all the hairs on my arms stand up in alarm. I'd mostly gotten over my post-Reginald Jones/Simon Butterman/ Santa paranoia, but the thought of someone else being in the house made me nervous. Taking my cellphone out of my pocket, I started down the stairs, being careful to avoid the spots I knew were creaky.

From the landing, I could smell smoke. Not the choking smoke of a house fire, but the faint tang of fireplace wood smoke. Two more steps and I smelled oranges. At the foot of the stairs, I could see the glow of a fire coming from the front parlor. Where there had been a great heap of garbage bags full of clothes, a little clearing had been made around the fireplace. Someone had torn open several bags full of furs, and laid the furs out in front of the hearth. Sitting in the middle of the fur nest was a bottle of wine and silver platter with some bread and cheese.

123

As I stood there marveling, he came up behind me. Silent where he walked on the hallway rug, then *clickety-click* on the hardwood floor. Silent again as he crossed the parlor rug to stand behind me. Close enough that I could smell him and feel the warmth of his breath.

"Glasses. I forgot the glasses," he said.

He wore his glamour when I turned around. Tall, dark, and handsome with an impressive beard. He held a pair of wine glasses in one hand. He reached for me, but I held up my hands to ward him off. I frowned at him and he frowned back.

"That's fine if you want to wear that for Gram," I said. "But I don't want you like that."

First the glamour went fuzzy around the edges. The space where his horns should have been shimmered and then the shoulders of his shirt sprouted hair. Abruptly, the whole mirage collapsed, and Peter stood before me exactly as I remembered him. The bead hung from his beard, still tied with blue silk thread. He was just the way I remembered him, except that he was here again. After three months. I wanted him to wonder, to make the first move without knowing what I would do, but I closed my eyes. An invitation. His beard tickled my chin, the bead bumping against my throat, and then his mouth was warm on mine. For a second, his tongue came out to tease against my lips, but as soon as my mouth opened and my tongue touched his, he pulled away from me.

First the glamour and now this. After three months, that was my hello kiss.

He knelt and set the glasses on the tray. After he poured wine into them, he turned to look up at me expectantly. "Come. Join me."

"I thought you weren't coming back," I said. I knew I sounded like I was about nine years old with hurt feelings.

"Not coming back? Why would you think such a thing?"

"I don't know. Maybe it was the part where you walked off without even saying good-bye."

He frowned and put his hands on my hips.

"I had many things to do. Many things that were left undone."

"I know." I knew. God, he'd been charmed for decades and decades. Of course, he had things he had to take care of that didn't involve me. "I just – I thought–"

"Ah, confess, confess."

"Confess what?"

He popped the button on my jeans open and snagged the zipper pull with one claw. I watched him drag it down. Watched that same claw sneak across my belly and up to the hem of my t-shirt. He pressed a kiss above my panties, and then his tongue darted into my belly button, leaving behind a shiver.

"You missed me. Confess that you missed me," he said.

"I just thought it was rude, walking off like that."

"Confess."

His thumbs eased into the belt loops of my jeans and abruptly jerked them to my knees.

"Confess," he said.

His thumbs returned to catch at the sides of my panties. He whisked them down just as quickly. It took him less than a minute to strip me naked and lay me back on the furs with a hot, eager kiss. It wasn't like I tried to stop him when he was peeling off my t-shirt and nipping at my bottom lip with his sharp teeth. He was still softer than any mink coat.

He might have said, "Confess," again but I couldn't really tell, because by then he had his face pressed between my thighs and his tongue was already proving its point, stroking and darting. His tail was like a semaphore, signaling to me when his tongue intended to caress and when it intended to strike.

"I missed you," I said.

He looked up at me and grinned. "Good girl."

Also by Red Hanner:

In the four hundred years since his marriage to Psyche fell apart, Cupid hasn't exactly been twiddling his thumbs. He moved to America, changed his name to C.C. Archer, and built the world's hottest online dating site. When reporter Tina Day crashes his New Year's Eve party, she gets more than the interview she was hoping for.

Archer may be passing himself off as a chubby, nearsighted jerk, but when Tina peels back the façade, she finds he's still the God of Love at heart. After he falls for her, she figures the relationship is going to be all roses and poetry, but Archer turns out to be more interested in leather belts and strap-on dildos, custom made for Tina.

Dating an ancient god is complicated. He won't let her turn on the bedroom light, but he knows how to do amazing things in the dark. Was that or wasn't that an extra tongue and a few too many pairs of hands? Just as Tina is figuring the relationship out, she and Archer run afoul of an ultra-conservative senator with a goddess on her side. The senator heads a group of religious zealots, who want to use Archer's website to promote traditional marriage. They're willing to do anything to convince him, and if Tina can't figure out how to stop the crazies, she may never get to use that strap-on.

Available for all e-readers now.

Paperback coming in January 2015.

About the Author

Red Hanner is a foul-mouthed troublemaker with a heart of base metal. Her goal is to write a whole series of seasonal erotica stories, starting off with *A Kiss from Krampus*, a dirty little romp with the Christmas devil, and *A Date with Cupid*, a tale of an ancient god getting his freak on. Future stories include Uncle Sam and Stingy Jack. Red believes that we need diverse books, and that means we need hot, smutty books by, for, and about people (and creatures) of all races, abilities, genders, and sexual proclivities.

You can catch up with her on Twitter @redhanner.

About the Krampus

To learn more about Krampus, you might check out his entry in Wikipedia, or visit Krampus.com, where you can send Krampus e-cards for the holidays. Also check out Monte Beauchamp's amazing collections of vintage Krampus postcards, available from most book retailers.